PROJECT ARMA

BODIE

NYSSA KATHRYN

BODIE

Copyright © 2021 Nyssa Kathryn Sitarenos

All rights reserved.

Cover by Dar Albert at Wicked Smart Designs
Edited by Kelli Collins
Proofread by Marla Esposito

❀ Created with Vellum

An enemy so fierce, disappearing is her only choice.

Maya Harper shouldn't be alive. All of her coworkers are dead, yet somehow, she survived. But now she knows something. Something important. Something that someone will kill to keep secret.

Running is her only choice. Her only protection. But no one can run forever, especially when the enemy's reach is long. Soon, trusting a stranger becomes her only option.

Former Navy SEAL Bodie Ryan is on a mission: Find Maya, a runaway lab technician—sole witness to a brutal crime—and keep her safe. She's become entangled with his nemesis, which makes Bodie and his team her only hope of living to see tomorrow.

Finding her is the easy part...separating professional from personal is the real challenge.

ACKNOWLEDGMENTS

Thank you, Kelli Collins, for always taking my manuscripts to the next level.

Thank you, Marla Esposito, for the eagle eye you cast over the manuscript.

Thank you to my wonderful readers for continuing to read my work and support this crazy author journey of mine.

Thank you to my husband and daughter. You make all this possible.

CHAPTER 1

*M*aya Harper's feet pounded the pavement. Cold air brushed across her face. The morning sun was only just rising over Keystone, Colorado.

This. This is what got her through the days. Through the hard, the uncertain, and the downright scary.

The exhilaration that rushed through Maya's body when she ran was like nothing else. The ache in her limbs was a welcome reminder that she was alive. That even though people hunted her, even though she'd watched a roomful of colleagues die, oxygen still flowed through her lungs. Her heart still beat in her chest.

Her damaged heart, that was. The one part of her that was simultaneously killing her, yet may have saved her life that fateful night.

Maya had to physically stop herself from pushing her body to move faster. Her doctor had advised her to slow down on her runs. Or at least cut back.

Atrial septal defect.

Or, in simpler terms, a hole in her heart. A hole that had been discovered a year ago when she'd started developing symptoms.

Lowered exercise tolerance, shortness of breath, fatigue,

fainting...a whole shopping list of problems that affected so many aspects of her life.

She should listen to her doctor's advice. She knew she should. But she'd lost so much in such a short period of time. She couldn't lose running as well. The one part of her day where she felt...normal.

Maya rounded a corner. There wasn't a soul in sight. It seemed to be the norm here. People in Keystone just weren't early risers. At least, she hadn't noticed them to be in the two weeks she'd been living here. It was probably due to the cold. It hit you in the face like a ton of bricks the moment you stepped out the door.

Unfortunately for Maya, the inside of the house she'd rented was pretty much the same temperature as the outside. So stepping out of the house didn't present a huge difference.

Maya had narrowed the reason for the cold house down to poor insulation and heating that only worked on rare occasions.

Being outside, on the move, was where she felt warmest.

She matched the swinging of her arms with the rhythm of her stride. The loud sounds of her feet hitting the pavement cut through the early morning quiet. So too did her quick breaths.

The coming months would be hard. Snow was almost due and the cold would no doubt be almost unbearable. But living in a cold house was much better than the alternative—living on the street.

Limited cash meant limited options. Not that she should be complaining. She was lucky she'd found a place in her budget.

If all went according to plan, she wouldn't be here for long. Just long enough to build up some savings and move on to the next town. Now that she had a job, she was able to breathe a little easier. A job that paid cash and didn't question her lack of ID.

Maya didn't know when she would feel safe enough to stop moving. There was a chance that day would never come.

She sucked in her next breath, feeling the familiar tightness in her chest. Some days it felt like there was a rubber band around her lungs, restricting her air.

Slowing to a walk, Maya lifted her hands and laced her fingers behind her head in an attempt to open her airways. To allow the oxygen to move through her lungs more deeply.

Breathe, Maya. In and out.

It was a familiar mantra. One she'd learned long before discovering her heart problem.

Breath was key, and not just when it came to running. When everything became too much, when the world felt like it was closing in on you, you breathed. Deep, controlled breaths that filled your whole chest. Then you kept going. You kept moving. You survived.

Maya was just about to pick up her pace again when a noise sounded behind her.

Footsteps, maybe?

Turning her head, she scanned the street. Still bare of people. The town was still tucked away inside their homes.

Just because she couldn't see anyone didn't mean no one was there though.

Was *he* there? The man who hunted her? The man who'd given the kill order?

Fear stabbed at her chest.

Maya had come to learn that people existed in this world who shouldn't. People who possessed unnatural strength and speed. And a desire to kill.

Closing her eyes, she fought to settle her ragged nerves.

One flicker of a sound. That was all it took to place her right back there, in that room, waiting to die.

You're safe, Maya. You're hidden.

The nightmares since that night had been unrelenting. But nightmares, she could handle. No one saw her terror in the darkness of the night.

It was when her memories crept into her conscious brain that was the problem. In broad daylight when people were watching. Her mind would try to convince her that she was back there. Back in that lab.

Shaking her head, Maya turned back to the path in front of her and started jogging again.

She switched her focus. Away from the things that were better kept buried, concentrating on placing one foot in front of the next. On exhausting her body.

Her pace was slower than she'd like, but if she pushed herself any harder, her heart would rebel. A year ago, she was faster. That was before the breathing issues. The heart palpitations.

Some days—the bad days—she wondered which would get her first, the damaged heart, the man who hunted her, or the loneliness.

At least she was used to the loneliness. Growing up, she'd bounced from one foster home to the next, only ever having herself to rely on.

Rustling noises from behind yanked Maya out of her thoughts, almost causing her to trip over her own feet.

Had she imagined that sound, too?

Without stopping, she glanced over her shoulder.

Again, there was nothing. Not a single soul in sight.

Still, fear clawed its way up her spine.

Moving her body faster, Maya breathed through the chest tightening. She ignored the fatigue and heaviness in her legs. On the worst days, she almost *hoped* her heart gave out first. At least then she would die on her own terms, right? And not at the hands of a killer.

No matter how hard she pushed her body though, she couldn't shake the feeling of being watched.

It was possible the noises were all in her head. Actually, it was incredibly likely. But that didn't stop the adrenaline from pumping through her system.

A memory of Paul being thrown across the lab flashed

through her mind. He'd hit the wall so hard, he died on impact. Then Josie. She'd been lifted off the floor as if she weighed nothing before the fingers around her neck had choked the life out of her.

Maya suppressed a whimper as she pushed her body even faster.

Steve's neck was snapped like a twig. Death had surrounded her. Terror paralyzed her.

Maya shook her head, trying to push the memories away. Trying and failing. They wouldn't leave her alone. There was no peace.

Maya was no longer jogging…she was sprinting. Pounding the pavement with every shred of energy she had. Irrational panic pumped through her veins, her heart almost beat through her chest.

Turning a corner, Maya screeched when she caught sight of the large man in front of her.

Digging her heels into the pavement, she came to a sudden standstill, only just stopping herself from colliding with him. Had she hit him, there was no doubt she would have bounced right off his big chest.

For a moment, neither of them spoke. The only sound was her ragged breaths. Her lungs were now desperate for air. Her chest rose and fell in unnaturally quick succession.

Maya tried to focus on the man. There was something familiar about his brown eyes, which stared so intensely into hers.

He was huge, towering over her five-foot-six frame. And he was all muscle.

Unease trickled down her spine.

She opened her mouth, but her breaths were now whooshing in and out of her body so fast that words were impossible. Even standing was beginning to feel like it required an insurmountable effort.

She needed to rest. To *breathe.*

Moving her hands to her head again, Maya tried to fill her lungs. It was hard. So damn hard. The combination of running and panic had taken everything from her. Her head felt light.

Involuntarily, she closed her eyes. Ice trickled into her veins. She'd let the fear get the better of her. Pushed her body too far. Now, she was a sitting duck. Waiting for the threat in front of her to act.

"Deep breaths."

Was that the stranger? His voice was different than she'd thought it would be. Softer.

Gentle hands touched her wrists, and her eyes snapped open. He slowly shifted her arms down.

"If you put your hands on your knees and bend over, the muscles around your lungs will be more relaxed. It will allow a more efficient exchange of oxygen. Help you breathe easier."

The lack of oxygen was causing more panic to surge through her chest. It was her struggle to breathe that kept her from questioning him or his motives.

The man guided her hands down until she took hold of her knees. Maya bent over and air began entering her lungs slowly.

"That's it. Deep breaths." His words were smooth and soothing. His voice like silk.

She focused on each individual breath.

His hand glided across her back. It was a touch that she should move away from. A touch that should incite unease.

It didn't. The warmth transferred from his hand, through the hoodie, to her skin, distracting her from the black dots that had started to cloud her vision. From the panic that had been suffocating her.

Maya didn't know how long she stayed like that. It might have been seconds but was more likely minutes.

Eventually, the band around her chest loosened. The dots in her vision receded.

Slowly, she straightened, and the hand fell from her back. She missed his touch immediately. Which sent spirals of confusion through her mind.

Maya took a step back, putting some distance between them. When she glanced up at him, it was to see he wore a mostly neutral expression on his face. He didn't look like he wanted to murder her on the spot. He just looked…normal. Worried, even.

Maya bit her bottom lip. "Thank you."

He dipped his head. "Little trick I learned from all the running I've done."

The fact that he was a runner didn't surprise Maya. He looked like one. He also looked like a weightlifter. And a boxer. Basically, he looked fit.

He tilted his head to the side. "You still look pale. Are you okay?"

No. She felt far from okay. Her entire body felt like it was in dire need of rest. The running and panic had stripped her of almost all energy.

"I'm okay." She couldn't be spilling her guts to a stranger. She shouldn't even be talking to him. "Thank you for your help."

The man smiled.

At the sight of his dimples, Maya suddenly remembered where she'd seen him. At the bar on Monday night. She'd dropped a tray of glasses and he'd been the only person to help her clean up.

"Bodie…" She breathed his name.

His smile widened, and the dimples deepened.

Maya's skin warmed. The man was good-looking, and when he smiled and those dimples formed, it was impossible not to notice.

"I thought you wouldn't remember me, Maya."

The sound of her name on his lips had her suppressing a shiver. "I'm not surprised you remember me…the clumsy bartender."

Stop, Maya. End the conversation. Walk away.

"I don't recall the clumsy part. I do remember you needing some help." He was watching her so closely, it was all Maya could do not to squirm. "It's your face that's hard to forget."

Maya only just managed to stop herself from lifting a hand to her face. It wasn't enough that he was looking at her with smoldering intensity; he had to say such sweet things too? All of it was having a strange effect on her insides.

Taking another step back, Maya wrapped her arms around her middle.

She really needed to walk away now.

Being alone was safe. She needed safety.

Maya hugged her waist a little tighter to ward off the cold. Now that she'd stopped moving, her skin had begun to chill.

"Well, thank you again, Bodie. This is the second time you've helped me."

"You're welcome, darlin'."

Heat returned to her cheeks at the endearment.

Smiling politely, she moved around him and started jogging again. She jogged slowly. So slowly that, had Bodie followed, he'd probably be able to walk alongside her.

Even though the deep breathing had loosened her chest, she still felt far from normal. When she got home, she'd rest until her shift at the bar. Rest and try to keep her mind from the danger that stalked her.

CHAPTER 2

"Tell me why I would hire you when you don't have a lick of bartending experience? I've already got one newbie, don't know that there's room for another."

Bodie gave Trish his best smile. The bar owner was, of course, referring to Maya as the new staff member. Maya was as inexperienced in serving drinks as they came. Just like Bodie.

He wasn't leaving this bar until Trish hired him though. Not a chance. He needed a reason to be around Maya. To protect her.

But that was a truth he wouldn't be sharing.

"Because it's coming into ski season, which is probably your busiest time of the year. Because the couple of times I've come in here, I've noticed that you're understaffed, and an extra worker who's learning the ropes is better than *no* extra worker." Bodie leaned over the bar. "Because I've served in the military, which means I can double as bar security. When customers get rowdy—which we both know happens often—and you need someone to kick them out, I'll be that person."

Bodie had been watching the bar for a week now. He knew that Trish only had two other bartenders helping her serve drinks and bus tables—Maya and a woman called Shayna. In the back, she had one cook who appeared far from capable of throwing out a group of rowdy men.

Bodie could see the older woman's mind ticking. He could also see an underlying respect for him, likely due to his mention of serving in the military.

Being good at reading people came in handy. Right now, he could see he'd almost won the woman over. Almost.

Trish leaned across the bar. "Say I did hire you. Your first night, a guy grabs one of my girls' asses. What do you do?"

What he'd *want* to do is tear the guy's arm off for touching a woman without her consent. And he wouldn't feel bad about it. Not for a second. But that wasn't the answer Trish was looking for.

"I'd give the asshole a chance to apologize. I'd wait three seconds for that apology to leave his mouth. If he chose not to, I'd ask him to leave. I'd ask nicely, but only once. If he chose wrong a second time, he'd be out of choices." Bodie's eyes hardened, and he looked Trish dead in the eye. "Then I'd make sure he left and didn't come back." *Using whatever means necessary.* "That night, or any other."

Bodie had no time for men who touched women without their permission. As far as he was concerned, they were the scum of the earth and needed to be taught a lesson. It would be his pleasure to be their teacher.

Trish flung the tea towel she'd been holding over her shoulder. The bar owner was in her mid-fifties, with curly hair that was only just being tamed by a hair band. There was a hardness to her.

The one time they'd spoken before, Trish had mentioned an asshole ex. He was sure that had helped create the hard exterior. He was also sure that the woman didn't tolerate crap.

Bodie liked that.

"Good answer."

Bingo.

"You get a trial run. Tonight. Thursdays aren't overly busy, but they're not quiet either. Come back at three, I'll show you how to make the most popular drinks before the crowd rolls in. If someone asks for a drink you can't make, call me over. Dress code is white shirt and jeans."

Bodie was already smiling. "Yes, ma'am. You won't regret it."

"I hope not."

Tapping the bar, Bodie gave Trish another smile before strolling out.

He breathed a sigh of satisfaction. The final part of the plan was in place. He'd set himself up in Keystone and was in the best position possible to achieve his goal.

He wouldn't be here forever. Just long enough to build a relationship with Maya, so that he could confide in her about who he was and how he could help keep her safe.

Pulling his phone out of his pocket, Bodie dialed his friend and teammate Wyatt.

Wyatt picked up on the first ring. "Red, how'd it go?"

Bodie smiled at the use of his nickname, one that only his team used. "I'm in. I start tonight."

"Good. Is everything else going to plan?"

Bodie ran a hand through his hair as he strolled back to his rental. "So far, so good. I hate that the apartment is a street away from hers. I'll have to spend a chunk of my nights watching her place from my car." He wished there was a way for him to remain close to Maya at all times. Unfortunately, he did need some sleep. Not much, but some. That meant there would be moments when she'd be unprotected. Working with her and watching her house when he could would have to suffice.

"I ran into Maya this morning on her run. She was skittish and scared." So damn scared. "I'm going to do what I can to gain her trust before I open up about how I can help."

There was something about the woman that had him wanting to fight all the evil in the world to keep her safe. It wasn't just the air of fragility that surrounded her. It was more than that. She desperately needed someone in her corner. Bodie had barely spent ten minutes with her, but he already knew that he wanted to be that person.

"And you're sure it wouldn't be easier to just tell her who you are from the start?"

Bodie had gone back and forth on that very question multiple times. Always coming to the same conclusion.

"The woman's terrified. She witnessed men use out-of-this-world strength, speed, and hearing. She watched them rob her workplace and kill her colleagues. Now she's running for her life." If she knew that he could do, what *they* could do, before she got to know him...no. He needed to build a relationship. "I'm sure she'll run if I don't do it this way."

He could only go with his gut on this. And his gut told him to gain her trust first. There wasn't a single part of Bodie that wanted to put *more* fear into the woman.

"I trust you to do what you think is best. I'm sorry it couldn't be me and Quinn there."

The team only knew about Maya because of Wyatt's partner, Quinn. She had been an investigative journalist for *The New York Times* when she'd stumbled across a series of lab break-ins. Maya had worked at one of the labs and been a witness to robbery and murder. She'd made contact with Quinn, confiding in her about what she'd seen.

Then Maya had disappeared, and Quinn had been kidnapped.

Even though his friend couldn't see him, Bodie shook his head. "After being kidnapped and having a damn bomb strapped to her chest, Quinn definitely needs time to rest."

"How long she'll stay here and rest is the question, though." Bodie chuckled when he heard Wyatt's sigh. "Anyway, let me know if you need anything else from me."

His chest warmed at his friend's words. Wyatt was one of his seven teammates. The eight of them had been on the same Navy

SEAL team. They'd also gone through Project Arma together. Been *changed* together.

Everything they'd gone through had created an unbreakable bond. The men on Bodie's team were his brothers. Together, they ran Marble Protection, a security and self-defense business, in Marble Falls, Texas. They also had a shared enemy.

Even though his friend couldn't see him, Bodie nodded. "Thank you, brother. I'll call if I need you. Stay safe."

"Right back at you."

Hanging up, Bodie continued walking to his rental.

The moment Bodie had arrived in town, he'd set up nearly undetectable silent alarms above her doors and windows. He'd also installed hidden cameras around the exterior. The moment someone attempted to enter her home, the silent alarm would trip, and he'd be able to view the video footage on his phone.

Bodie smiled at an elderly couple who walked past. He hadn't met many people in Keystone yet. But those he had met were friendly.

That was good. He needed friendly. To take his mind off all the ugly in the world. In particular, one man who kept evading capture. The man responsible for Project Arma, the program that had changed Bodie. Made him stronger. Faster. That had changed every facet of his life.

Hylar.

The team had managed to weaken him, but so far, they hadn't been able to take him down.

For a moment, Bodie wondered if Maya had discovered anything about Project Arma. The men who had broken into the pharmaceutical company had demonstrated their abilities. But was that all she knew? That men like him existed?

A part of Bodie suspected there was something else the former lab technician was hiding. Call it a hunch. What, exactly, he wasn't sure. But he definitely wanted to find out. He hoped that soon, she would trust him enough to tell him. He also wanted to get to know her better. Who she'd been before she'd become a woman on the run.

He had no idea why he *wanted* to know. Maybe because his friends kept finding love. Five of the eight of them now had partners. They were changed men. Better men. He saw the way his friends looked at their women. Like they were the centers of their worlds. Like they would walk over fire to protect them.

Bodie couldn't help but want the same. Want to feel that love and connection. Want someone to depend on him, who he could depend on right back. And he was definitely attracted to Maya. Felt their chemistry the first time they'd met.

Shaking his head, he entered his apartment building. Even if he did find someone to love—Maya or otherwise—there was no guarantee that love would be reciprocated. If there was anything he'd learned in his thirty-two years, it was that *nothing* in life was guaranteed.

Not love. Not trust. Not even tomorrow.

The best anyone could do was follow their instincts and hope they led to a semblance of happiness.

Bodie shut the door of his newly rented apartment. The place was fully furnished, small but comfortable. There were two bedrooms, two bathrooms, and everything was fairly new. Not that any of that mattered to him. His mission was all that mattered.

To an outsider, Bodie protecting Maya without her knowledge may seem strange. To him, it was necessary. Most people didn't know the danger that lurked in the world. It creeped in the shadows, rarely presenting itself until it was too late.

Being a Navy SEAL, Bodie had been exposed to a lot of that danger. Hylar being the worst. Hell, the man had his own sister killed not even a month ago. He had no morals. No heart.

If Hylar's men were searching for Maya, wanting her dead, she didn't stand a chance on her own. Bodie would be her *only* chance. And he took his new job as her protector very seriously.

CHAPTER 3

*M*aya rushed down the street toward Inwood Bar. She was ten minutes late.

Argh. She couldn't believe she'd fallen asleep.

Well, that wasn't entirely true. She *could* believe it. After all, she'd barely slept for weeks. It was only a matter of time before she crashed.

But, heck, she wished she'd at least set an alarm when she'd shut her eyes on the couch. It would have saved her from having to throw on her work clothes like a lunatic and all but sprint to the bar.

Dammit. She was already a below-par bartender. Add being late to the mix and why *wouldn't* Trish fire her?

Maya couldn't afford to lose her job. No one else in town was hiring and moving was expensive.

The very idea of that happening had a tremor of unease coursing down her spine.

Reaching Inwood, Maya rushed through the front door, immediately catching sight of Trish behind the bar. The owner was mixing drinks for some regulars. She looked over at Maya and gave her a smile.

She returned the smile, followed by what she hoped was an apologetic look. A please-for-the-love-of-god-don't-fire-me look.

The other woman gave her a nod before turning back to the drinks.

Did that mean she wasn't mad? Maya wasn't an expert on reading people but Trish appeared okay. Maybe that meant *she* would be okay. The place wasn't too busy, so perhaps the other woman would be lenient.

Beelining for the back room, Maya had only taken one step inside when her feet abruptly came to a stop.

A man stood in front of her. A shirtless man. A shirtless man facing her with cords upon cords of muscles spanning his tanned chest.

Maya's mouth went dry. The guy had the most perfect body she'd ever seen.

When her gaze rose to his face, she found herself staring into a set of familiar brown eyes. Not familiar because she knew the man. Far from it. Familiar because his intense stare had clashed with her own not nine hours ago.

A smile curved his lips. It did nothing to slow her beating heart. "Maya. We meet again."

Maya swallowed, trying to wet her throat. "What are you doing here?"

Only staff were allowed in this room. It held a small couch, a round table, and cubbies for staff to leave their belongings. Unless he planned to rob one of the workers, she couldn't think of why he would be back here.

Bodie pulled a white shirt over his head. She hadn't even realized he'd been holding it. The muscles in his thick arms bunched and the ones on his chest rippled.

Oh, sweet Jesus, the man was built like a Greek god.

Once the shirt was in place, it stuck to his body like a second skin. Showing off every hard ridge of muscle.

It probably would have been polite for Maya to look away. But the very idea of doing so seemed impossible.

"Sorry. I spilled a drink on my last shirt. Luckily, I brought a spare." His voice was deep, making the hairs on her arms stand on end. "To answer your question, Trish just hired me to work behind the bar, so you'll be seeing quite a bit more of me."

He was working here? With her?

"I thought…I mean, I didn't know Trish was hiring."

God, she couldn't even get her words out.

Bodie lifted a shoulder. "Maybe she took pity on me. A man passing through town, begging for a job."

Her brows lifted. The man's circumstances had quite a resemblance to her own.

He took a step forward, and Maya's heart skipped a beat. This close, she was breathing his scent. His woodsy, all-male scent that made her want to lean closer.

Was it strange that she had a sudden urge to run her hands down his chest?

He tilted his head to the side. "I should get out there."

Oh…she was blocking his exit. While she'd been mauling him with her eyes, he'd been waiting to get out.

Heat rushed to her cheeks in embarrassment. "Sorry."

Maya took hurried steps to move aside. Unfortunately, in her haste, her feet somehow tangled with each other, and she almost toppled over. *Would* have toppled over had Bodie's hands not shot out to grab her arms.

"Whoa, you okay, darlin'?"

His fingers fully encircled her arm. His hands warm and firm on her skin.

Okay? No, she wasn't okay. Her head was at war with her libido. It was as if the sight of a shirtless man, *this* shirtless man, had short-circuited her brain. Either that or turned the thing to mush.

Mentally shaking her head, Maya gently pulled her arms free. Bodie released her immediately. "I'm okay. Thank you."

One side of his mouth lifted, showing one of his delicious dimples. "I'll see you out there."

He gave her a wink before leaving the room. A wink that had her stomach doing somersaults. Maya spent the next ten seconds standing there, trying to calm her overheated body.

What the heck was going on? Yes, the man was attractive. Probably the most attractive guy she'd ever laid eyes on. But did that mean she should turn into a blubbering mess?

She gently touched the tops of her arms where his hands had been.

Glancing around the small room, Maya's eyes paused on the clock. Crap! She was now fifteen minutes late for her shift.

Crap, crap, crap.

Shoving her bag into one of the cubbies, Maya quickly dashed out to the front.

Trish was standing in almost the exact spot she'd been when Maya entered. Only now, Bodie stood beside her. Trish was helping him mix a drink.

Moving to stand on Trish's other side, Maya wrung her hands while she waited for her to turn in her direction. When she did, Maya gave another apologetic smile. "I am so sorry I'm late. It won't happen again."

She felt like she should offer the woman some kind of explanation, but the only one she had was that she'd taken a nap that ran long. Then, after already being late, she'd spent another five minutes ogling the new employee.

Yeah, no. Maya wouldn't be offering Trish an explanation.

Trish shot a look at her watch before turning back to Maya. "Only fifteen minutes, hon. Don't sweat it. These things happen."

A long, relieved sigh released from Maya's chest, the tight band of worry loosening.

Good. She wasn't fired. She wouldn't be on the street. Not today, anyway.

Trish leaned closer. "I think your shirt's inside out."

Maya's eyes dropped to her shirt. Darn it, it was. She'd barely spared herself a look in the mirror before rushing out the door.

Trish chuckled. "The amount of time's I've done that..." She turned back to Bodie, while Maya ran to the staff room and fixed the shirt.

Good lord, what a miserable afternoon.

Maya returned to the bar and began serving drinks. She slipped into the role of bartender quickly, even though the job in no way came easy to her. She was a scientist. Her jobs during high school and college had all been in tutoring. This was a new world to her. And she was as far from a natural at it as one could get.

In a way, that was kind of good. It meant she had to really focus on the tasks at hand. Focus on what she was pouring into the glasses, on balancing them on the tray. It took all of her attention, meaning there was no time to think about other stuff. People who might be searching for her. Atrocities she'd witnessed. Health problems.

At least, that was usually the case. Tonight, she was focused on something else. Or rather, *someone*. Every so often, Bodie would brush close behind her. Or ask a question in his sexy-as-sin voice. One time, he reached across her body for a bottle of whiskey. His arm had brushed her stomach and caused a spike of awareness to course through her core.

It was a *big* distraction.

Sneaking a glance beside her, she saw him unscrew a cap off a beer. His biceps rippled. Heat washed over her torso.

"You got a new fella?"

Maya's gaze flew to the man in front of her, a smile already curving her lips.

Roe was a regular at the bar and had been Maya's first

customer. He was there each and every night, always sitting on the same stool.

He'd mentioned that he was a retired police officer, but she never would have guessed. He had a gentleness about him.

She grabbed a glass and filled it with his favorite beer. "If you mean, did Trish hire a new fella? Then the answer is yes. His name is Bodie."

She could see Roe inspecting Bodie as she pushed the beer across the bar, his easygoing air dimming as he studied the other man with assessing eyes. His expression remained like that for a few seconds before he nodded in what looked to be approval.

"Good. It's about time Trish hired some muscle around here. You women are too vulnerable."

Working in this bar was actually the safest Maya had felt in quite a while. She almost felt camouflaged amongst the crowd.

"I haven't seen too many people who would warrant 'muscle.'"

Not in Keystone, anyway. In New York, she'd seen a different type of muscle. A muscle that was far from normal.

Roe's features hardened. "Erring on the side of caution is always smart. You never know what's going to pop up on a normal day at work."

Ice trickled down Maya's back at his words. She knew that better than anybody. She'd lived it. She definitely hadn't expected people to walk into her lab and kill every colleague on shift.

Maya nodded. "It'll be nice having him around."

Giving Roe one last smile, Maya turned to the next customer. She tried to force her mind off his words. Off the memories they evoked. But no matter how hard she tried, she couldn't distract herself.

You never know what's going to pop up on a normal day at work.

She still remembered the conversation she'd been having with Belinda moments before her friend had died. They'd been discussing the other woman's teapots.

Belinda had been describing her collection. Apparently, she had a lot. She'd even invited Maya over to see them.

Maya had laughed. She would've been all too happy to spend time with the other woman. Friendships were in short supply. Unfortunately, she'd never had a chance to accept the invitation.

For a moment, Maya stopped what she was doing. Pushing back the memories that came next. Of what happened to Belinda moments later.

Sometimes it was easy to suppress them. Today, for some reason, it was a lot harder. The ugliness crept into her mind and clouded every other thought.

Suddenly, a body brushed against her back. A hard, warm body.

Her gaze swung up and clashed with Bodie's. He was reaching for something above her head. His lips stretched into a smile that went all the way to his eyes.

"Sorry, darlin', just grabbing a new bottle of whiskey."

She returned his smile. She couldn't not. "Bottles are also kept under the counter down at the other end."

If possible, his smiled widened. "I know." Then he leaned down, his breath brushing against her neck. "But you were over here."

Her abdomen heated at his words. So did her cheeks.

She watched him stroll back to where he'd been preparing drinks. Every other thought in her mind ceased. She'd been right about one thing. Bodie was one big, fat distraction. From work. And from everything else.

CHAPTER 4

*B*odie locked the bar door.

It was his sixth night working at Inwood, but his first night closing with Maya. Shayna was supposed to close with her tonight, but Bodie had managed to convince the woman to swap with him. If she hadn't, he would have just hung around, skulking in the shadows, keeping an eye on Maya. This was easier. Also warmer.

Bodie grabbed glasses from tables on his way back to the bar, his gaze shooting to Maya wiping down the counter. "You think Trish is nervous about the two new kids in town doing the close?"

Maya lifted her head and smiled. "I think Trish was a step away from closing the bar down early to avoid this very situation."

Bodie chuckled. "We'll just have to be the best damn bar closers around so she builds some trust in us."

A small frown creased Maya's brow. It was cute. "And what would the best damn bar closers look like?"

Bodie carried half a dozen glasses to the sink. "Sparkling

floors. Glasses so shiny a person can see their reflection. Maybe 'good morning' spelled out with nuts on the counter."

Maya's lyrical laugh caused Bodie to pause mid-step. The strain she wore on her face like a mask lifted briefly. The little stress lines around her eyes smoothed out.

"Beautiful." He murmured the word quietly. So quietly that it would never reach her ears.

For the next ten minutes, Bodie and Maya worked in silence. Silence for Maya, that was. For Bodie, the sound of her steps, her breaths, even her heartbeat, were loud and clear.

Most of the time, Maya's heartbeat sounded just like everyone else's. There were also times that it didn't. Every so often, there was a whooshing sound from her heart, unlike anything he'd ever heard.

Had he not known about her heart defect, he would have been concerned.

Atrial septal defect—a hole in the wall between her atria. He'd researched it extensively before meeting her, so he knew that sometimes the defect required surgery. Sometimes it didn't. It depended the size of the hole. Bodie had no idea which category Maya fell into.

"The other morning when I saw you on your run, you were quite out of breath. Does that happen often?"

Maya's head popped up from the table she was wiping. A rosy pink tinged her cheeks. "No. It doesn't happen often." She paused, as though she were considering her next words. "I have this heart thing. I'm still getting used to it. I pushed myself too hard that morning."

"A heart thing sounds serious."

Maya lifted a shoulder like it was nothing. "I'm okay."

Bodie was keenly aware she had carefully avoided confirming or denying the "serious" part of his statement.

He could have found out the full extent of Maya's medical history himself. Well, not himself, but with the help of Wyatt.

Wyatt was a whiz with technology and could find out a lot with the click of a button. That's why the team called him Jobs. He'd already done a background check on Maya, but had carefully avoided looking into the woman's medical history.

It had seemed like too much of an overstep. She wasn't an enemy. So if she wanted to share, that decision should be up to her.

Bodie only knew about Maya's heart condition because of Wyatt's partner, Quinn.

"Bodie?" His gaze shot across the room to Maya. She had stopped cleaning altogether and was watching him. "Are you still thinking about my heart?" She sounded curious, but there was also a tinge of confusion.

Damn. He should have masked his features better. Unlike his brothers, he was never one to conceal his emotions too thoroughly. "Is it so bad that I'm worried about you?"

Her expression softened. "You don't know me."

Oh, but he felt like he did. She felt familiar to him. "We've worked together for a week. I probably know you better than you think."

She gave a small laugh. "It would take a lot longer than a week to get to know me."

Wasn't that true for everyone? "Tell me something about you then. Something true. Something not many people know."

"You first."

Easy. "I believe in love and happy ever after's. I believe everyone deserves someone by their side to make the bad days bearable and the good days even better."

God knows he could have used someone to make his bad days more bearable after Project Arma had been uncovered. Plus, he'd seen love firsthand. The impact that it has on a person. He almost craved it.

The pulse on the side of Maya's neck sped up. "I've never loved anyone before. Never had anyone love me."

Thick silence filled the air. Every protective instinct in Bodie sprang to life. He wanted to simultaneously hurt every person in Maya's past who was supposed to love her and didn't, and pull the woman into his arms and promise that love would come.

Maya scrubbed a hand over her face. "I shouldn't have told you that. I don't know why, but I feel like I can say things to you that I wouldn't normally say."

Good. Bodie wanted her to talk to him. "Every person who's touched your life and *not* loved you is a fool."

Her eyes widened. "Maybe I'm just not the kind of person people love."

Anger shot through Bodie like wildfire. Nothing about what she'd just said was true. He was in front of her in an instant. Reaching out, running his knuckle down her cheek. So damn soft. "You are."

Two words. And he meant them.

She opened her mouth, and Bodie got a sudden urge to kiss her. Taste the beautiful woman in front of him.

Then she blinked. Once. Twice. Three times...before looking away.

She gave a little shake of her head. "We should keep going."

They should. Only there was a part of him that wanted to remain exactly where he was. A large part of him.

MAYA REACHED FOR HER JACKET, all the while avoiding Bodie's gaze.

She couldn't believe what she'd said to him. She'd only known the man for a week and already she was showing him the broken fragments of her heart.

What the heck was wrong with her?

The one small reprieve was that she hadn't mentioned the

danger she was in. Telling him no one loved her? Okay. But not that she was on the run and hiding…a wanted woman.

When his knuckle had touched her cheek, it sent tingles of awareness through her entire body. The urge to reach up and kiss him had almost been overwhelming.

Luckily, she'd saved herself from doing just that. Nothing could come of it. And there was a good chance she'd never have lived down the embarrassment.

"Ready to go?"

Jeez, even his voice made her toes curl. Maya nodded and trailed behind him, watching as he locked the door. "I'll see you tomorrow."

Bodie shook his head. "I was raised to be a gentleman and gentlemen walk women home, *especially* after dark."

Maya glanced down the street, then back to Bodie. "How do you know I don't have a car?"

"Do you?"

No. And she *would* feel safer with Bodie by her side. But she wasn't his responsibility. "I don't. But you don't have to walk me home."

His answer was immediate and firm. "I insist."

She wrapped her arms around her waist to ward off the cold. "Okay. Thanks." It really would be nice to have someone big and capable with her. She indicated to the right with her head. "I'm this way."

Bodie walked beside her, his legs so long it took about two of hers for every one of his. "You don't have a warmer jacket?"

She wished. Unfortunately, just about everything she had, she'd bought along the way. Because money was short, so too were everyday essentials. Like weather-appropriate jackets. "I don't, but I'm fine."

If fine meant freezing her butt off.

Maya wasn't sure if it was her imagination, but she almost

thought she heard a soft growl beside her. "I wish I'd brought a jacket I could give you. I don't feel the cold too much."

Bodie was still wearing his white shirt with no jacket over the top. Just looking at him made her cold. It was like forty degrees...freezing!

She felt him edge closer, causing his shoulder to brush against hers. His warmth immediately penetrated through her thin jacket to her skin.

"So, what brought you to Keystone?" Maya asked. The man intrigued her, and she found herself wanting to learn more about him. Even though she shouldn't.

There was a pause. It was slight, but enough to make her look up. Under the moonlight, it was hard to interpret his expression.

"The decision to come here was last minute. I guess you could say something drew me. I'm not sure how long I'll be staying."

That was very cryptic. Not that Maya minded. She had her own secrets, so he was allowed his. "Me either."

If finances weren't a problem, she'd already be gone. Even though she felt safe in the busy bar, and the money was very welcome, staying still made her nervous. It gave people a chance to track her.

As they walked, she anxiously waited for him to ask her what *she* was doing in Keystone. She'd told Trish she was just passing through. Exploring the country.

For some reason, she didn't want to lie to Bodie.

"Are you enjoying it here?"

She just stopped herself from expelling a relieved sigh. It wasn't the question she was expecting, and she was grateful. "The locals are nice. The people at work are friendly. So, yeah, I'm enjoying it."

As much as she could while continually glancing over her shoulder.

His big shoulder gently nudged hers. "But one person you work with is particularly nice, isn't he? Quite the looker too."

One side of Maya's lips pulled up. "Yeah, Rodney in the kitchen is super lovely and very good-looking." All two hundred and fifty pounds of him. And they weren't pounds of muscle.

Bodie chuckled. It was low and sexy and had her body tightening. Christ, was there anything that *wasn't* sexy about this man?

As they continued to walk, Bodie charmed Maya with his conversation, temporarily making her forget about the cold as well as everything else that wasn't quite right in her life. When they reached her front door, Maya realized she hadn't smiled or laughed as much as she had with Bodie since...before.

"Thank you for walking me home."

He dipped his head. "You're welcome. Would you mind if I gave you my number?"

Maya's brows shot up in surprise before Bodie continued.

"I'm assuming you live alone. I'm also assuming that being new in town, you don't know many people. If I give you my number, you'll have someone to call if you need anything. Even if it's just a friend."

"And you're my friend?"

His tone lowered. "I'd like to be."

Oh, boy.

Maya nibbled on her bottom lip. It wouldn't hurt. She was beginning to trust him. She'd only known him for a week, but so far, he'd been nothing but kind. He was warm and easygoing. When she talked, he really listened. And any time he touched her...

A shiver coursed down her spine even *thinking* about his touch.

Having the number of someone she trusted sounded nice.

Maya pulled out her phone—her burner phone—before handing it to Bodie. He keyed in his number and then handed it back.

"Good night, Maya."

She expected him to walk away. He didn't. At least, not

straight away. Instead, he leaned down and pressed his lips to her cheek.

Maya didn't move. She didn't so much as breathe. His lips were soft and warm and made lava pool in her stomach.

When he lifted his head, he gave her a smile. "I'll see you tomorrow, darlin'."

Then he was gone.

Maya continued to stand there for a good thirty seconds, watching him walk away. Her hand went to her cheek, lightly grazing the place his lips had just touched.

Yep. She was in trouble. She shouldn't be building relationships with people. Relationships that would be hard to break when she soon left.

Shaking her head, Maya unlocked her door and pushed it open, careful to step over the thin thread she'd strung near the ground. Luckily, there was a small gap between the door and floor, which made her system work.

Still in place and unbroken.

Next, Maya systematically went through the house, checking the string on every window as well as the back door. The place was small, with a kitchen and living area to the right, and doors leading to the single bedroom and bathroom to the left.

None of the threads were broken. That meant no intruders.

She was safe.

The process caused Maya to crash back to reality with a thud.

Danger still lurked. She wasn't safe. She wouldn't be safe for a long time. And it would be best not to drag Bodie into her hell.

CHAPTER 5

*M*aya woke to the morning sun peeking through the curtains. She instinctively snuggled farther into the blankets.

Holy crap, it was freezing.

The first thing she'd done when she'd stepped inside last night —after checking her string security system, of course—was say a little prayer that the heating would work before switching it on. When it had, she'd just about dropped to her knees in relief. It had been cold. Much too cold to sleep without it. It was only a wall unit, but because the house was small, it was pretty effective at heating the whole place.

Clearly, the thing had decided to stop working during the night.

Maybe she'd just stay under the blankets until her shift at the bar. Tempting, but unfortunately she would require food at some point.

Her stomach chose that moment to growl.

Argh, okay. She needed to get up. She also needed to grab some groceries, because she was pretty sure her cupboards were completely barren.

Scrubbing her eyes, she tried to work up the courage to climb out of bed. At least she was wearing socks, so her toes wouldn't freeze. Before moving to Keystone, she'd never realized how cold floorboards could get.

Really cold.

Sitting up, the blanket dropping to her waist, Maya rubbed her arms. Goose bumps were already forming on her skin.

Okay, definitely too cold to step straight outside for her jog. She doubted her heart would let her reach the speed she'd need to get sufficiently warm. Maybe she'd have a quick, hot shower first. Or maybe a long one. Maybe the longest one in history.

Gritting her teeth, she climbed out of bed and shuffled to the bathroom. She cursed the whole way there. What she wouldn't give to still be in her cozy, warm New York apartment right now.

Maya turned on the hot shower tap and waited for the water to heat. No way was she getting undressed first. The other morning, the water had taken a good sixty seconds to heat up. That may not sound like long for some, but when you were standing in an igloo-like house, it felt like a damn eternity.

She was pretty sure she'd actually turn to ice if that happened today.

A minute passed, and the temperature didn't change. Then another.

It wasn't until after five full minutes of nothing but icy-cold running water that Maya finally accepted she wasn't going to get her hot shower.

Darn it to hell. No heating and no hot water left her with a very cold home. Just another thing to go wrong in the Maya Harper chronicles.

Closing her eyes, Maya breathed in a calming breath. Falling apart wouldn't help. She needed to focus on finding a solution.

She could contact the landlord; after all, he should be the one fixing any problems with the place. But when he'd given her the key, he'd wanted to see her ID. She'd told the guy she was waiting for a replacement. If she called him, there was a good chance he'd ask to see it again.

So, no. That was not an option.

She couldn't afford to hire a professional to come look at the heating or hot water. Not even close.

Moving back to the bedroom, she rummaged through the dresser drawer for her warmest sweater. As she pulled it out, her gaze caught on her phone, which was sitting on top. Her mind quickly flicked back to Bodie giving her his number the previous night.

Was there a chance he might be able to look at either the hot water or heating? Some people were really handy at home maintenance.

Shaking her head, she quickly dismissed that idea. She couldn't call him. She'd known the guy for a week, she couldn't be asking him for favors.

Once she was dressed in leggings and a sweater, Maya made her way to the kitchen. A hot drink before her run was her last resort. She'd just switched the kettle on when she noticed her breaths were coming out in soft wheezes.

Stopping what she was doing, she put her hand to her chest.

Crap. Was the cold affecting her heart?

Maybe she'd just call Bodie and ask if he could help. What was the worst that could happen? He could say no. Sure, she'd be a bit embarrassed, but at least she would have tried.

Grabbing her phone, Maya hit dial before she could talk herself out of it.

He answered straightaway. "Bodie speaking."

He sounded wide awake.

Maya bit her lip as she worked up the courage to talk. "Bodie. It's Maya. Sorry to call so early."

"You don't need to apologize, darlin'. That's why I gave you my number."

Heat filled her cheeks. She would never tire of hearing him

use that endearment. "I was actually wondering if…if you had any experience with fixing hot water or heaters? If you don't, that's completely fine…"

Maya would freeze her butt off, but she'd survive.

"I'll pop over now."

Maya's jaw dropped at the speed with which he agreed to help. "Are you sure? If you're busy, I don't want to disrupt you—"

"Not busy in the slightest. Give me five minutes."

"Okay, um, thanks."

Hanging up, Maya quickly made the bed and tidied the few things that were laying around. Not that she had much.

She also removed the thread from the bottom of the front door. Even though it was very unlikely he'd see it, she felt better with it out of the way. Like her secret was safer.

BODIE TWISTED the pipe back into place before turning around to face Maya. Even though he'd told her she could leave him to it, she'd continued to pop back into the bathroom every five minutes to offer assistance.

He'd fixed the heating first simply because she'd looked absolutely freezing. It pissed him off to no end that she'd been living in such subpar conditions. The place was unquestionably a dump. He didn't like her living here one bit. Unfortunately, he didn't really have a choice in the matter.

"All fixed."

Her mouth dropped open. "Really? Just like that?"

Bodie chuckled. The woman clearly had no faith in him. Either that, or she was so relieved she was in shock.

"Just like that. There were no big issues. Just small things that the landlord should have, but clearly hadn't been, maintaining. Did you give him a call?"

Maya's eyes darted to the ground, giving Bodie the answer before she'd said anything.

"Um, he didn't answer when I called."

That was a lie. The avoidance of eye contact and hitch in her breath gave her away. Not that Bodie would be calling her out on it. He had a feeling he knew why she hadn't called the landlord. And it had everything to do with her not wanting to bring attention to herself. When on the run, a person's goal was to be forgotten and invisible.

Maya looked up again. "Thank you for coming. I know we haven't known each other for very long, but I was a bit desperate. Mostly because of this heart thing of mine."

Bodie took a step closer. "Are you okay?"

He knew from his own research that almost half of atrial septal defects close on their own. But if they didn't, if symptoms worsened and the hole was too big, surgery was required. He'd been hoping Maya's defect fell into the former category. But her symptoms were pointing more and more toward the latter.

She lifted a shoulder. "I'm managing."

That wasn't an answer. Before Bodie could comment on it, Maya turned and headed toward the living room. He followed.

"Sorry, I only had instant coffee," Maya said over her shoulder. "I know the stuff tastes terrible."

It tasted like cardboard. Not that he cared. He'd had worse. "It wasn't so bad," he lied. "I appreciated the coffee. Are you going for a run?"

A small frown marred her brow as she glanced out the window. "I am. It's a bit later than I would usually go, but," she lifted a shoulder, "I'm addicted. You know that high you get from running? That's the best part of my day."

Bodie *did* know about the high from running. The kick of endorphins could be epic. But he wouldn't go so far as to say it was the best part of his day. Particularly not over the last week.

"I haven't been on my run either. Care for some company?"

He almost laughed at the way her brows shot up. Her mouth opened and closed twice before speaking. "You want to run with me?"

He sure did. Not only was it the easiest way to keep an eye on her, but he also worried about her heart. Particularly after he'd found her out of breath and about to pass out the previous week.

The woman would already know that she shouldn't be running so much, but sometimes people were irrational. He had a feeling this was Maya's way of trying not to lose the last semblance of her old life.

"If that's okay with you?"

"I'm not very quick. I used to be faster…" She shook her head. "That's a bit irrelevant. What I mean is, you look like you could run circles around me."

Bodie was quick enough to run circles around literally everyone but his teammates, but he wouldn't be admitting that just yet. "It's not so much about the speed than it is the company for me. Please. Put a lonely guy out of his misery. Give me a running friend."

Maya nibbled on her lip. "Okay."

Triumph.

As Bodie waited for Maya to slip on her shoes, he subtly scanned the living room window. There was a thread running along the base. Very similar to the one he'd seen on the bathroom window.

When he shifted his attention to the front door, he noticed there was nothing there. Perhaps she'd had thread on the base of the door but removed it for him.

Clearly, Maya was trying to watch for intruders. If they came while she wasn't home, a broken string would tell her.

Unfortunately, if those intruders were men from Project Arma, a broken thread wouldn't give her the heads up she was hoping for. By the time she noticed, it would already be too late.

She was smart. She'd know that. It was probably the only thing she could think to do to help her feel safe.

Maya stood. "Ready?"

Bodie smiled at her and they headed outside.

The sun was now higher in the sky, taking the edge off the cold. Good. He hated the idea of her running in such icy weather. As they started to move, he felt the energy shift in her immediately. The rigidity in her limbs visibly lessened, and the tension faded from her face.

She almost looked like she was at peace.

Bodie had watched her run before. He knew she loved it. This was where she felt free.

"You enjoy running?" He already knew the answer, but he wanted to hear it from her.

"I love it. Always have. Any time my life's gotten hard, running has been my escape. The part of my day where I can push my body to exhaustion. Forget the bad."

"It's freeing," Bodie added.

She glanced at him, looking almost surprised at his words. "So freeing. And invigorating and calming."

"The endorphin kick you mentioned doesn't hurt either."

"Very true. I'm always a nicer person after a run."

"And I'm always a lot better looking," Bodie joked.

Maya chuckled. "I don't think you *could* get better looking."

She snapped her mouth shut as soon as the words were out. This time Bodie chuckled. She clearly hadn't meant to say that out loud. He loved that she had.

"You know, I try to tell people that very thing and it rarely goes down well."

Maya threw her head back and laughed.

Bodie's entire body tightened at the sight. He wouldn't be surprised if he ran into a tree with how little he was focusing on the path in front of him. The woman beside him was radiant when she laughed. He wanted to see more of this side of her.

"Thank you," she said softly.

Confused, Bodie's brows pulled together. "For what?"

"Helping me feel human again."

CHAPTER 6

*M*aya's gaze flicked across the bar toward Bodie for what had to be the tenth time that night. She needed to stop. They were only an hour into their shift, for heaven's sake.

Why was she so drawn to him? Actually, she knew the answer to that. And it wasn't just his perfectly chiseled body. It was his gentleness and his humor and the way he was able to make her feel comfortable so easily.

Basically, the guy was one huge heartthrob.

Fortunately, he hadn't noticed her looking his way. Not yet. Or maybe he had and was being polite by not bringing attention to it.

Argh, she hoped not.

When the next customer asked for a beer, she grabbed a glass and began filling it from the tap.

The place was packed. It was like everyone from the area had decided tonight was the night to stop at Inwood Bar.

"Cute, isn't he?"

Swinging her head around, Maya saw Shayna standing right beside her. The other woman was stunning with her platinum-blond hair and long, toned legs. They hadn't spoken a lot since Maya had begun working there, but so far, the other bartender seemed friendly enough.

"Who?"

She knew who. But playing dumb seemed the safest option.

Shayna rolled her eyes. "Uh, the new tower of hunk that's been hired to work with us. Don't pretend you haven't been checking out that six-pack. And just look at those arms, they're like tree trunks on steroids."

Maya had looked at them plenty. It was impossible *not* to check them out, what with the thin cotton of his white shirt stretched so tightly across his biceps. The material just about threatened to tear apart.

"He's okay." If okay meant drop-dead gorgeous.

The frown on Shayna's face told Maya she wasn't buying her casualness for a second. "Girl, don't you lie to me. I know you're seeing what I'm seeing. There is nothing *okay* about that man. He's all sex and power and heat. And that's not even touching on how capable those former-military hands look."

Maya almost spilled the beer she was pouring before setting it down. "Former military?"

Shayna lifted a shoulder. "He hasn't said it, but I've dated tons of military guys. They all have the same physique and 'yes ma'am' etiquette."

Maya pushed the beer across to the customer before taking his money. She turned her gaze back to Bodie. It hadn't crossed her mind that he could be ex-military. Now that she thought about it, that made sense. Not that it mattered to her one way or the other.

Shayna leaned closer. "Every time you look away, he looks directly at you."

Bodie was looking at her? No. That couldn't be the case. *She* was the one obsessed with *him*.

Shayna slapped Maya's ass before walking away with a grin,

causing her to jump. Shaking her head, she moved to the next customer.

Shayna was very different from Maya. Probably her exact opposite. But she was nice enough and easy to talk to. That description fit most people in Keystone. She'd spent more time working with Trish than Shayna. The bar owner was upfront and honest. She was also friendly and seemed to want to help Maya.

She had no idea why. She was a stranger to Trish. Yet, she'd given her a job and seemed okay with the fact she'd taken a while to settle into it.

Spotting Roe at his usual stool, Maya moved to stand in front of him. "The usual?"

Roe nodded. "You know it. Busy one tonight."

Maya grabbed a glass, thanking her lucky stars that she was finally feeling semi-confident in her ability to serve drinks without making mistakes. "This has to be all of Keystone, right?"

Roe chuckled. "If that were the case, my ex-wife would be here chewing my ass out."

Maya placed the beer in front of him. "You have an ex-wife in Keystone?"

"Yes, ma'am. The only woman in the area who can't stand me."

This time Maya laughed. "I can't see how any woman wouldn't love you."

"Just her." Roe took a sip of the beer. "Don't get me wrong, we were happy once. We just grew out of love."

Maya's smile dimmed. "I'm sorry."

He shrugged, not looking sorry at all. "It happens. It's called life. No use crying over it. Tell me, you got a man to take care of you?"

As if her eyes had a mind of their own, they immediately sought out Bodie. He was serving drinks down at the other end of the bar. The women across from him looked like they belonged on the cover of magazines. Skintight dresses. Faces without a single blemish. Legs for days.

Swallowing, she turned back to Roe. "No. No man."

"Good. Being single gives you a chance to know who you are first."

She had a pretty good idea of who she was...Maya Harper. Geeky. Alone. Good at science and remaining hidden.

She kept her voice light. "Have you always been this wise, Roe?"

He leaned back in his seat. "Always."

Shaking her head, Maya chatted with him for a few minutes before turning to another customer.

Over the next hour, Maya moved as quickly as she could. She alternated between serving behind the bar and clearing tables. Hopefully, that meant she would sleep well tonight. Pass out from pure exhaustion. The very idea of getting a solid night's sleep seemed too good to be true.

"Woah, slow down, darlin'."

Maya jumped at the deep voice that spoke into her ear. She'd been moving toward the back tables and hadn't even noticed him.

Turning, she saw Bodie standing less than a foot away.

"Sorry, was I moving too fast?"

Just like he had the other day, Bodie lifted a hand and grazed his finger across her cheek. It made her momentarily forget about the busy bar around them. The job at hand.

She could get used to these casual touches of his.

"I just don't want you to overdo it."

His gaze was intense and completely fixed on her. Heat spiraled through her body.

Then she remembered that he knew about her heart condition and probably didn't want her passing out on him.

"Thank you. I'm okay. I just—"

Before Maya could finish what she was saying, her attention caught on the television behind Bodie. Police were on the screen, congregating outside a building.

Maya's breath caught as she searched the faces of the officers. Searched the faces of the men *around* the officers.

Hell, she didn't even know what the man who hunted her looked like. All she knew was his voice. The voice of the man who'd given the kill order.

"Hey."

Maya's gaze shot back to Bodie. A worried expression had come over his face. He was now standing even closer than he'd been before. The bar was packed, and there were dozens of people to serve, but still Bodie waited.

Shaking her head, she took a step back. They both needed to get back to work.

"Sorry. My mind drifted for a moment. I'm okay. Thank you for checking on me."

Stepping away, Maya continued to the back of the room. While the others served at the bar, she would continue to clear tables. It would provide her with the few minutes she needed to get out of her head.

She hadn't told another soul she was running. *Who* she was running from. After surviving the break-in, she'd just wanted to disappear. It was all she could think of to remain safe. She hadn't told anyone where she was. Although, someone knew that she was alive. One woman. A journalist named Quinn.

Maya had been scared and alone. When the email from Quinn had popped up, asking for information about the break-in, Maya had reacted on instinct.

Creating a new email address and writing back, she'd told Quinn about what she'd seen. She'd done it out of duty. Hoping the other woman could make people aware. Stop it from happening again.

After some emails back and forth, Maya had begun to trust her. Christ, she'd even met her to tell Quinn the story in person.

She'd left one thing out, though. One very important detail.

"Hey, sexy, want to get me a drink?"

Pulling herself out of her thoughts, Maya glanced at the booth beside the table she was clearing. Four men sat there, looking her way.

Maya wasn't sure which man had spoken. It could have been any of them. But they all looked like jerks. "Orders are taken at the bar."

She'd taken a step toward the counter when a strong hand wrapped around her arm and yanked her in the opposite direction.

"Come on now. You're right here."

The feel of his fingers digging into her skin had her heart crashing against her ribs. "Let go of me." She said the words firmly.

He and his friends chuckled. "Okay."

He let go of her arm, but that same hand quickly snaked around her waist and pulled her onto his lap.

The tray dropped from her fingers and clattered to the ground.

"Is this better?"

Maya sucked in a quick breath, panic bubbling inside her chest. She pushed at his chest, only to have his arm tighten around her.

"I've been watching you," he continued, ignoring her struggle to get up. "Not just tonight. Since you began working here. Thought I'd finally introduce myself."

Repulsion slammed into her gut at the feel of his hot breath on her neck.

Maya opened her mouth to tell him to release her but before she could utter a word, Bodie's hands slammed onto the table. The loud bang echoed through the bar, silencing most conversations.

Fury rolled off him in waves. "You have five seconds to release her."

She felt the man below her tense. If possible, more rage

contorted Bodie's face. She almost wanted to pull away from *him* as well.

"And if I don't?"

Dear god. The man either had a death wish or was too drunk to recognize the very real threat in front of him. Even though the man was sitting, she could tell Bodie was a heck of a lot bigger. In both height and breadth. He also looked ready to kill.

Fear fluttered in her stomach.

Bodie leaned closer. "I break your arm."

Maya's lungs seized. Her heart was now pounding against her ribs. She didn't want to see a fight break out. And she certainly didn't want to get in the middle of one.

For a moment, the hand around her waist tightened.

Then it released her.

Maya quickly jumped away from him. The moment she was on her feet, Bodie wrapped gentle fingers around her arm and pulled her behind him.

"Now, apologize to the woman and get out."

The man scoffed. "I'm not doing either."

Could he get any dumber?

With lightning reflexes, Bodie grabbed the guy's arm and yanked him from the booth. Maya was right. Bodie towered over him. He dragged the guy behind him like a rag doll.

"Let go of me!"

Bodie didn't let go; he marched the guy right over to the door and outside.

When the door slammed shut behind them, Maya stood there, unsure of what to do. She didn't dare move a muscle. Neither did the rest of the men in the booth.

After a minute, she began to worry. Bodie was taking too long to have just chucked him outside. Which meant he was either threatening him with more bodily harm, or actually *causing* him harm.

Swallowing, Maya was about to lift the tray from the floor

when Bodie stepped back inside. The angry scowl was still firmly in place. He marched straight back to the table.

"You three—out."

The men glanced around at each other, as if deciding whether to do as he asked.

Oh, gosh. Please go!

Eventually, they came to their senses and left. A whoosh of air escaped her chest.

When the men had exited, Bodie gently took hold of her arm again and led her toward the break room.

BODIE WAS ONLY JUST CONTAINING his rage. The moment the asshole had put his hand on Maya, he'd seen red. If there hadn't been so many people around, he would have been able to make it to her faster. A lot faster.

It had taken too much time. The asshole shouldn't have been able to pull her onto his lap. To wrap his arm around her waist.

Pulling her into the back room, Bodie closed the door after them. When he turned around, he noticed how pale she was. He could also hear that her heart was racing a million miles an hour.

Using every shred of effort he possessed, Bodie smoothed his features and soothed his voice. "Are you okay?"

Maya wrapped her arms around her waist. It was a defensive gesture. And it made Bodie want to walk right back out and punch the asshole a second time.

"I'm okay. I mean, all he did was grab me."

There was no "all he did" about it. The man had crossed a line. Touched her without her permission and invaded her space. Maya had already experienced enough trauma. He was sure even the smallest form of violence could trigger a great deal of fear in her.

"I'm sorry it took me so long to get to you." He wanted to kick his own ass.

Her eyes widened. "Oh, it's not your fault. You don't need to apologize."

He felt like he did. "It won't happen again."

The color began coming back to Maya's cheeks as she stepped close and placed her hand on his chest. "Bodie. I'm not your responsibility. But I'm so grateful for your help tonight."

Placing his hand over hers, he gave a small smile. He in no way felt calmer about the situation. He still wanted to chase the assholes down. But, for now, he was okay with the knowledge Maya seemed relatively okay.

Her health was his priority. Even if she didn't know it yet.

"Are you sure you're okay?"

Rather than answering straightaway, she did something that surprised the hell out of him. Reaching up on her toes, she pulled his head down with her free hand and pressed a kiss to his cheek.

"Thank you for your help, Bodie. Tonight, and every other time you've saved me."

Then she released him and left the room.

Bodie stood there for another second, remembering the warmth of her lips on his skin. The sweet breath of the woman who was quickly working her way past his defenses.

CHAPTER 7

*M*aya wrung her hands together as she watched the trees pass through the bus window.

Disappointment sat like a brick in her gut. So too did frustration and agitation. It had taken her three buses and half the day to travel to Cheyenne. All for one hour's use of a public computer to research *him*.

She wanted a face. A face to put to the voice. She *needed* a face, so every person she saw wasn't an enemy until she heard them speak. Every man wasn't the man who gave the order to kill Maya and her colleagues.

She hadn't found a face. She'd found diddly squat. As far as the internet was concerned, he didn't exist.

It wasn't just him she couldn't find any information on; it was also *them*. The men who were too strong and too fast to be human.

Maybe they *weren't* human. After all, what kind of human could hear a person's heart beating in their chest?

She wasn't surprised she couldn't find any information. If the government knew of their existence, no way would they let the public know. It would cause mass panic and hysteria. Especially if the public saw the men do what she'd seen.

Maya hadn't exactly needed to travel all the way to Cheyenne to use a public computer. But doing the research as far from home as possible made her feel safer. After all, there was always the chance the search could alert someone to her location.

Was that possible? She had no idea. She'd seen it done in movies, so it wasn't crazy to think it could happen in real life.

Maya watched as the sun tried to peek through the clouds. It was coming to the end of another cold and cloudy day. It was her first day off in a while and she'd spent it on a bus, with nothing to show for her travel.

It was annoying.

Her stomach rumbled, reminding her that she hadn't eaten all day. Now that she thought about it, other than a box of cereal and some almost-expired milk, her kitchen was empty.

Luckily, it was at that moment she spotted the sign welcoming them to Keystone. Good, the next stop would be the grocery store. She still didn't have a lot of money. Heck, she had basically none. But she couldn't very well starve.

The other night, Maya had treated herself to meat and vegetables for dinner. It had been her first meal that wasn't built on carbs in a while. It was heaven. And her body had immediately thanked her for it.

As the bus rolled to a stop, Maya grabbed her bag and stepped out.

The wind had her hunching her shoulders and hugging her arms around her waist. Damn Keystone and its frosty wind. She should be used to the cold after living in New York City, but she'd had weather appropriate clothing there. This was a shock to her system.

Stepping into the grocery store, Maya grabbed a basket.

In the last few months, she'd become good at scouring stores for specials. She didn't buy for recipes, she bought whatever was cheap that she could turn into a meal. The foods didn't always match, and sometimes the combinations tasted downright strange, but unfortunately, being low on money meant you didn't have the luxury of being picky.

Starting with the fresh produce section, Maya beelined for the broccoli, which had a big "special" tag. She then systematically went through the store, grabbing every bargain she could find.

Now that she had a semi-permanent place to live, frozen vegetables seemed the smartest choice. Not only were they cheaper, but she could buy in bulk and they kept for ages.

Maya had just stepped into the last aisle when she stopped in her tracks. There, standing in front of the cereal, was Bodie.

Only he wasn't wearing his usual smile. He held no groceries; instead, he had a phone to his ear. There was a frustrated, almost angry expression on his face.

When his gaze clashed with hers, the frustration cleared, replaced with...surprise?

Crap. Bodie had messaged her today. Twice! And she'd ignored both texts.

Not intentionally, she'd just been focused on other things. Namely, identifying the faceless voice. Bodie was too much of a tall, dark, and handsome distraction.

"I CAN'T FIND HER ANYWHERE." Bodie ran his free hand through his hair as he spoke to his friend Luca on the phone. It was taking every shred of his energy to remain calm. "I should have put the goddamn tracker on her phone already."

"Red, you said yourself that when the silent alarm went off, you watched her leave. She didn't have a packed bag to indicate she was skipping town and she didn't appear scared. Evie is doing what she can to hack into street surveillance, but there isn't a lot of it around Maya's house."

Bodie blew out a frustrated breath. He'd rushed over to Maya's house the moment he'd watched the camera feed and saw her stepping outside. She was already out of sight when he arrived. Keystone was a small town, and she hadn't been wearing workout clothes, but he'd checked her normal running path anyway. There'd been no sign of her.

Next, Bodie had called the bar, hoping she'd been asked to get some stuff done for Trish. She hadn't been there, either.

He'd messaged her twice, but had received no response.

Where the hell was she?

His teammate Luca was engaged to a woman who was excellent with technology. Bodie had been on and off the phone with them all day, him searching the area in person, them through local video surveillance around town. So far, Evie had found nothing.

Bodie had just been wandering the streets and shops of Keystone for most of the day, searching for the woman like a blind man.

Jesus, this was bad.

Now he was checking the grocery store one last time. Then he planned to camp out at her house overnight. He prayed that she wasn't lost.

"Yes! Found her."

Bodie jerked at the sound of Evie's voice in the background.

"Where?" he asked, stopping in the cereal aisle. When he looked up—the air whooshed out of his lungs.

There, standing less than ten feet away, was the woman he was searching for. The woman he'd been hoping and praying to find.

"Never mind. I found her, too," Bodie said quietly, hanging up and shoving his phone into his pocket. Clearing his features, he moved toward her. "Hey, darlin'. Wasn't expecting to see you here."

He kept his voice calm. A hell of a lot calmer than he felt.

She gave him a small smile as she lifted her basket. "Just getting some groceries." She glanced at his hands. "You don't have anything."

"I only came in for one thing." *You.*

She shot a glance at the shelves, then looked back at him. "Cereal?"

Hell no. He was not a fan of the stuff. Never had been, never would be. "Have dinner with me."

The request hadn't been premeditated. More a desperate solution to keep the woman close. Reassure himself that she was safe and alive, and he hadn't failed her.

Maya's expression flicked from surprised to unsure. "I've already got some groceries—"

"Your place isn't far. We can drop them off, then head out for dinner. There's a new burger joint around the corner that's supposed to be good."

Her eyes lit up. The flecks of gold in her pupils brightened. He was pretty sure it was because he'd said the word "burger."

Maya nibbled on her lip. Like she was yearning to say yes, but something held her back.

"Please." He needed to tip the scales in his favor here. "Save me from my own company. I'll pay, and I also promise, no bad jokes."

Well, he promised to *try* for no bad jokes. He always found them funny, it was others who didn't.

"Okay."

Bodie just stopped himself from sagging in relief. Not only would he get to spend time with the intriguing woman, he'd also be able to insert a tracking device into her phone. Something that would have saved him a great deal of stress today.

Maybe she'd even tell him where she'd been.

CHAPTER 8

*M*aya took a bite of her burger. A huge bite that should have had her feeling embarrassed. It didn't. The burger was the best-tasting thing she'd eaten in months. The delicious flavors woke up her deprived taste buds, reminding her that good food did exist.

When she looked across to Bodie, it was to see him staring at her, a ghost of a smile on his lips. Still, she couldn't feel embarrassed. She was too happy.

"Sorry." She said the word with a full mouth.

"Don't apologize. I'm glad I chose the right spot for dinner."

Any spot that wasn't her kitchen would have been the right spot. "You did. This burger is amazing."

So too was the company. Before the burger had arrived, she hadn't been able to take her eyes off the guy.

Bodie took a bite of his own burger. She wouldn't say he looked as consumed by the burger as she was, but he also didn't look like he was hating it.

"So, tell me, what did you get up to on your day off?"

Maya paused, a fry halfway to her lips. Her brain scrambled to come up with a lie. "I, ah, just spent the day at home. Slept in, watched some TV. Nothing special." She hated lying. And it didn't help that she was terrible at it.

Maya wasn't sure if it was her imagination, but she almost thought she saw disappointment cross his features. If she had, it was fleeting. Before she could think too much on it, a smile stretched his lips. "Lazy days are the best. You can just switch off from the outside world and live in your bubble."

Unfortunately, it was almost impossible for Maya to switch off from the outside world. Although, while she was with Bodie, she was pretty damn close.

His phone lit up on the table. He glanced at the screen before turning it over. Suddenly, Maya was reminded of the fact that she'd never responded to his messages.

Crap. He hadn't even asked about them.

"I'm sorry I never texted you back today. I didn't look at my phone much. I wasn't trying to ignore you."

He popped a fry into his mouth before lifting a shoulder. "It's okay. Trish has been matching our shifts, so I knew you were off with me. I was just interested in knowing what you were up to. Now I know."

Only he didn't. Not really.

"Now you know," she murmured quietly, kind of wishing she could tell him the truth.

Offloading her secret to him would be nice. It would also be incredibly selfish, seeing as she'd be putting his life at risk. The only reason she'd shared part of her story with Quinn was because the woman had been so persistent. Not to mention that as a journalist, she was in a position to warn people.

Taking another bite of her burger, she realized it didn't taste quite so amazing anymore.

"Tell me about yourself. Any siblings?" he asked.

Oh, boy. Maya hated family questions. After all, who enjoyed sharing information on an upbringing that was less than perfect?

"I don't remember my parents. They died when I was really young, and I grew up in and out of foster homes."

The fact that she didn't have a family used to cause an ache in her chest. When she was younger, she would see kids with their parents and wish she had what they did.

That didn't happen anymore. She'd learned that life wasn't fair. The sooner she'd accepted that, the quicker she'd been able to shift into survival mode.

The pity she was expecting to see from Bodie didn't come. If anything, his features remained neutral. "That would have been hard."

"It was."

Some of the homes had been less than ideal. Absentee care-givers, alcohol abuse…one of the foster mothers had even been violent. Maya didn't like to think about that.

Being with good families was almost as tragic, though. Because her time with them always came to an end.

"The loneliness was hard," she continued, swirling a fry around her plate. "Families couldn't always keep me because their circumstances would change. It meant I had to move around. I changed schools a lot. Creating lasting relationships was impossible."

This time, the sympathy she was expecting was there, but for some reason, she didn't hate it as much as she thought she would.

"I'm sorry."

She lifted a shoulder. "It made me work harder at school. I was academic and my grades were something I could control." Her brain was the one thing she knew would save her once she'd aged out of the system.

"What did you do after high school?"

Casting her eyes down, she debated over what to tell him. The truth was, she'd won a scholarship to study science at Dartmouth University. But admitting that would raise too many questions. Questions she didn't want to answer.

Forcing a smile, she looked back up. "Hang on a sec, buddy, it's your turn."

Bodie didn't appear annoyed in the slightest that she hadn't answered his question.

"Sure. I grew up in Jacksonville. My parents still live there, happily married. I have an older brother and sister."

"Ah, youngest of three. That explains it."

He chuckled. It was a deep, masculine chuckle that had her stomach quivering. "If you mean that you're not surprised my parents stopped with me because I'm perfect, then you'd be correct."

She couldn't stop her own laugh. "No. I mean it explains your boyish personality. Your humor."

Bodie leaned forward. "But mostly my faultlessness, right?"

Maya's smile broadened. God, the guy was something else. She never smiled as much as when she was with him.

Throughout the next half hour, Bodie continued to make Maya smile and laugh while she resumed her meal. Her hard day had definitely turned around.

"That was amazing," Maya said, popping the last fry into her mouth. "Thank you for dinner."

"Thank you for joining me." He started pushing his chair back. "I'll walk you home."

Maya wasn't going to argue with him. "I'll just use the bathroom first."

When Maya stood, she was surprised to see Bodie standing, too. She had no idea that men still did that.

So, he was a gentleman and good-looking. And funny. And smart. And just about every other positive trait she could think of. Jeez, she was in trouble.

As Maya walked past him, she was almost certain she felt the light brush of his touch on her hip...probably wishful thinking.

She used the bathroom quickly before washing her hands. When she looked at her reflection in the mirror, she noticed that the person staring back at her looked completely different than the person she'd seen in the mirror a few weeks ago.

There was color in her cheeks, and the anxiety-ridden expression was nowhere to be seen. She almost looked happy. Maya hadn't looked or felt that way in a long time.

Smiling, she started to grab her phone out of her back pocket, only to stop when it wasn't there. What the heck? Had it fallen out?

Darn it. She hoped not. She didn't want to have to buy *another* burner phone. Not so soon, anyway. This one was almost brand-new.

Heading back to the table, she breathed out a long sigh of relief when she saw it sitting beside her empty plate. "I thought I'd lost my phone for a minute," Maya said, shaking her head. "I didn't even realize I'd taken it out."

Bodie smiled as he stood beside her. "I'm glad you didn't lose it. I'd have to convince you to give me your number again."

Maya almost scoffed. Yeah, like that would take much convincing.

When Bodie held his jacket open for her, she just stared at it blankly. "What are you doing?"

God, the man probably thought she was simple. It was obvious what he was doing. What she really wanted to know was *why* he was giving her his jacket.

"Your jacket isn't warm enough, and it's a ten-minute walk back to your place."

She opened her mouth to say no but Bodie was already stepping forward. Hesitantly, Maya slid her arms through the sleeves.

Holy jam on a cracker, the thing was *so* warm. And even better, it smelled just like the man in front of her.

Stepping outside, they began walking back to her place. When his hand reached for hers, she almost jumped out of her skin.

"It's dark," he said quietly by way of explanation. "I'd feel better holding your hand."

Maya threaded her fingers through his. His hand was like a mini heater. And it pulsed awareness all the way up her arm and through her body.

Along the way, Bodie asked Maya a few more questions about herself. Questions that were mostly safe. The questions that she couldn't answer, she successfully managed to dodge or give half-truths. Half-truths would be easier to remember.

"What's something that attracted you to Keystone?" Bodie asked as they turned onto her street.

Other than the safety and anonymity? There was one other thing.

"Ice skating."

She could feel Bodie's eyes on her. He was no doubt surprised.

Maya continued before Bodie could ask. "I've never been. You know how you watch a movie where a woman ice skates and she looks so happy?" *And free.* "It made me want to try it."

While living in New York, she'd walked past Rockefeller Center more times than she cared to remember. Not once had she stopped and skated. She was going to make that a priority while she was here in Keystone.

If there was anything this last month had taught her, it was that life is short.

Bodie's hand tightened around hers. "What a great idea."

They came to a stop outside her door. The only light was the reflection from the moon. It was dim. Almost romantic.

"Thank you for tonight." Yet again, he'd made her feel normal. Something that was so far out of reach so much of the time.

"Thank *you*. It was the best night I've had in a while."

Maya was sure he was exaggerating. The compliment still made heat fill her cheeks. Sliding her key into the door, she pushed it open but didn't move to step inside yet. "I'll see you tomorrow?"

His gaze was still fixed on her face, studying her with the usual intensity that she'd grown used to. "You will."

When he leaned his head down, Maya held her breath and didn't move a muscle. She just waited to see where his lips would land.

When they touched her cheek, she sighed.

"I'll see you tomorrow, Maya. Lock the door after yourself."

Plastering a smile to her lips, she nodded and stepped inside. She shouldn't have expected a kiss. She'd only known the guy a short amount of time.

Then why was disappointment bearing down so heavily on her chest?

$\mathcal{A}$s Maya opened a container of peanuts, she couldn't for the life of her figure out why anyone would eat from snack bowls at a bar. All she could think of was dirty fingers rifling through them, touching every single one.

Nope. Not Maya. She was a germaphobe through and through. Spending most of her adult life working in a lab, she'd learned just how quickly germs and bacteria spread.

One of the first science experiments she could remember doing involved swabbing half a dozen items and growing the bacteria in petri dishes. The copious colonies of bacteria that had grown from swabbing a keyboard alone had disgusted her. After that, sanitizer had become her best friend.

This was actually the first year in the last eight that Maya *wasn't* working in a lab. And she missed it. Science had always been her strength. In school, when she felt disconnected from the world, being shifted from foster home to foster home, science had been her constant. The thing she excelled at.

She missed that feeling. Of being accomplished. Capable.

A little voice in the back of her mind reminded Maya that there was a possibility she might never get back to that job…that life. There was a chance that this running and hiding and working in whatever job was available could be forever.

"You fill that bowl any higher and our customers will have more than a snack."

At Trish's words, Maya was pulled out of her thoughts, noticing the overflowing dish of peanuts in front of her. Darn it! "Sorry, Trish."

Like she needed to give her boss *another* reminder that she was the worst bartender in Keystone.

Trish shrugged. "A few lost nuts aren't going to cost me my livelihood, hon. Don't stress."

How did she do that? Be such an amazing boss? No matter how many mistakes Maya made—and there had been a few—the other woman never seemed to get frustrated or angry.

The bar owner moved to the next table, refilling the napkins. "I didn't always own this bar. There was a time when I was just a bartender here, too. If I told you the number of mistakes I made when I first started, you'd be shocked."

"You? Make mistakes?" Maya teased.

"Oh, yeah. I was a hot mess. I came in, begged for a job, even though I had no idea what the job entailed. Hell, I'd barely stepped foot in a bar before that day." Sounded exactly like Maya. "I'd never done much of any work. But that wasn't the main reason I was terrible at the job. I was terrible because I was distracted."

Maya swallowed as a hard look came over Trish's face. There was also a glint of anger in her eyes.

"I was running from a man who treated me like his personal punching bag. I was scared, always looking over my shoulder, waiting for him to find me and kill me."

Maya sucked in a quick breath. The strong, hard woman in front of her was someone Maya would never pick as being a victim. "I had no idea," she said quietly.

Trish nodded. "Everyone's got a past. Some are just worse than others."

That was for sure. "Did he find you?"

The other woman chuckled. It was devoid of humor. "Of course. Didn't take him long, either."

Maya tried not to react to Trish's words, but they hit too close to home. *Of course.* Like it was inevitable. Like the evil that stalked a person would always find its victim.

A chill crept down Maya's spine.

"But by then, I was ready for him," Trish continued. "I was stronger. I wasn't afraid to use whatever means necessary to protect myself. And, I had friends then. Friends who would back me up."

Maya went back to filling the bowls, but her mind was ticking with Trish's words. She made it sound easy...winning...*surviving*.

The problem was, where Trish's ex was likely a normal civilian, Maya's enemy was anything but. He had a far reach. He was a man of authority with strong men to fight his battles.

Maya snuck another peek at Trish. "What happened?"

"He attacked me." Trish said the words so casually. Like it wasn't one of the most terrifying moments of her life, which Maya was sure it would have been. "He hurt me." Trish looked Maya dead in the eye. "I fought back. My friend Mick heard what was happening and helped. My ex was arrested, and I told him if he ever came near me again, I'd shoot his dick off. Haven't seen the bastard since."

If Trish's words weren't so chilling, Maya might have laughed at the threat she gave her ex. But she had to ask. "Would you? Shoot him if he came back?"

"Hell yes, I would. I meant what I said and he knew it." Trish placed napkins on the last table before crossing the room. She stopped in front of Maya. "There are shit people out there who can make us feel like victims. Like we have to leave the world we know to survive. But we all have the right to feel safe. And sometimes, it's up to us to remind the assholes."

Trish knew.

Not the exact story. Not that Maya's enemy was a faceless man with killers in his pockets...but she knew something.

That was why she'd hired Maya. Kept her on even though she made one lousy bartender. It shouldn't surprise her. She'd shown up in town with no ID, no money, and probably reeking of desperation.

"I think you're telling me to fight back," Maya said softly, knowing there was no point in denying she was running. "But I don't think I would win that fight."

In fact, Maya was almost certain she would lose. The price would be her life.

Trish leaned closer. "I'm telling you to survive first, but when the time comes, and it usually does, you use whatever means necessary to live."

Ice filtered into Maya's limbs. *When the time comes.*

Other than hiding, she had no means of surviving. She didn't even know if it was possible to survive against her enemy. Instead of telling that to Trish, instead of admitting that if she was found, she was dead, she forced a small smile to her lips. "Thank you."

Trish opened her mouth, but before she could say anything else, the door to the bar opened. Looking up, Maya saw Bodie enter, looking just like he always looked...tall, dark, and so damn sexy.

"Afternoon, ladies."

His gaze flicked from Trish to Maya. It remained on Maya for a moment longer than normal.

Heat washed over her torso before she gave the man a small smile.

Lord, she needed to get ahold of herself.

Turning back to her task, Maya filled the final bowl before

heading to the kitchen. The bar was set to open in five minutes. Hopefully, it was busy again and she could focus on work. She would *not* spend the entire evening staring at Bodie. Nor would she be letting their almost kiss from the previous night occupy her thoughts.

Okay, technically, it *was* a kiss. Just not the kiss Maya wanted. Not the one she'd been expecting when his head had lowered.

She'd been so sure his lips were going to touch hers…her entire body had tingled with anticipation. Only they didn't. He'd pressed another kiss to her cheek. Similar to a kiss from a friend. Because that's what Bodie was. A friend.

Shaking her head, she busied herself in the kitchen for a couple of minutes, deliberately waiting until she heard the sound of customers out front before joining Bodie and Trish.

Over the next few hours, the bar steadily filled with people, and time passed quickly. Unfortunately, there were still too many moments when Maya wanted to look in Bodie's direction. When her eyes wanted to track him, see that smile stretch across his lips.

But she didn't. Even though it took every little scrap of self-control she had, she didn't look his way once. She almost felt like she deserved a medal.

"Maya, help an old man out and hydrate me."

She smiled at Roe across the bar. "Hate to break this to you, Roe, but beer isn't actually all that hydrating."

Roe put his hand to his chest. "I have so little in my life. Why do you need to hurt me with these truths?"

Maya laughed, grabbing his beer. She'd grown fond of the older man and genuinely looked forward to seeing him each night. Roe never failed to bring a smile to her lips.

"How's the boy doing?"

Boy? Bodie wasn't a boy. He was all man, and her ovaries knew it.

Maya almost looked over at him. Almost.

"He's doing good. He certainly slipped into the role of bartender a lot smoother than me. We both have zilch in the way of experience, but he's obviously a faster learner." She pushed the beer over to Roe.

"Nonsense. You're my favorite bartender here." He frowned. "But don't go telling Trish or Shayna that."

Maya shook her head. "You're too kind, Roe. Not that I believe you."

He took a drink of his beer. "I only speak the truth." He leaned over the counter. "But remember, not a word to the other women."

Because Roe undoubtedly told them the same thing.

"I'm a vault. Let me know if you need another." Smiling, she moved from behind the bar and headed out to clear some tables. She swore she heard the older man scoff. Probably because he never had just one. It was always a few. Not that Maya was judging him. She was sure he'd worked hard his whole life, and if this was how he wanted to enjoy his retirement, then it was no one else's business.

Arriving at the back corner table, Maya began clearing the glasses. The corner was quieter than the rest of the room, and she welcomed it. Working in a noisy bar was often a shock to her system, and something she'd really yet to get used to. It was the furthest thing from the quiet lab.

Maya was stacking glasses, listening to the background chatter, when something caused her to stop moving.

A voice. A voice so familiar, it had her stomach cramping.

Spinning around, she frantically searched the faces around her, expecting to see someone looking at her. Watching. Waiting to take her.

But there was no one looking her way.

Placing the glasses back on the table, Maya listened. Had she really just heard it or had the voice been in her head? She focused all her energy on the sounds in the bar, praying she wouldn't hear it again. That she hadn't heard it in the first place.

There was no familiar voice. Nothing to pull her attention. But her heart still hammered in her chest. Her breaths were still short.

The room suddenly felt too crowded, but she couldn't help but continue to scan the people around her. She wasn't sure what she was looking for. Maybe for someone's gaze to clash with hers. A look on someone's face that told her to run.

Her heart continued to pound. His voice was now a whisper in her head. Those same words she'd heard him speak that night on repeat.

Kill them. All of them.

Shaking her head, she tried to push it away. The problem was, every man she saw was starting to look like an enemy. Every face was the face of a killer.

Because giving a kill order made you a killer, right?

Maya tried closing her eyes, but the moment she did, she was back there. Back in that lab, watching her friends be murdered. Waiting her turn.

It was the only time in her life she'd wished for death. Because surely being dead was better than *anticipating* death. Knowing your turn was moments away.

A whimper escaped her lips. So soft, it would be lost in the noise of the room. Similar to the whimper that had escaped her lips *that* day. The one that made the murderer look her way. Look her way and smile like he enjoyed her fear.

Her chest constricted.

A hand pressed to her shoulder, and she jerked.

Was it him? The man who'd been on the phone? Or was it them—the men doing his killing?

A soft voice spoke in her ear. A voice so different to the one in her head.

"You're okay, Maya. You're in Keystone. You're safe."

Safe.

She wasn't in New York. She wasn't in the lab watching her friends die. She was here, at Inwood Bar, and Bodie was speaking to her.

She tried slowing her breaths—oh god, did she try—but her airways weren't cooperating. She wasn't sure if it was her heart or her panic that was the problem. Probably both. But she was suffocating.

An arm wrapped around her waist, pulling her away from the people. Pulling her toward silence.

CHAPTER 10

*B*odie kept Maya in his line of sight as he served the man in front of him. He knew the exact moment something went wrong. Even though she had her back to him, he saw her muscles visibly tense. Her body go unusually still.

Bodie placed the EFTPOS machine down and gave Maya his full attention. What just happened?

When she turned around, dread pooled in Bodie's gut. Her face was pasty white. She almost looked like she could topple over right where she stood. It wasn't just the shade of her skin that alarmed him, it was also the expression on her face.

Raw panic.

Bodie took his eyes off her for a moment to scan the crowd, looking for threats. Anyone who looked out of place. He didn't find a thing. In fact, no one was paying her the slightest bit of attention.

Trish, who had been serving a few feet away from him, moved to his side. Her eyes also across the room on Maya.

He couldn't hear her heart rate over the music and sound of the crowd, but he could see the pulse at the base of her neck pounding. She was scared. Of what, he wasn't sure.

"Go," Trish said quietly. "Help her. Shayna and I have the bar covered."

Giving a small nod, Bodie rounded the bar, reaching her just in time to hear a whimper from her lips. It damn near tore his chest in two.

Placing a light hand on her shoulder, he immediately felt her body jerk. Bodie leaned down and placed his lips at her ear.

"You're okay, Maya. You're in Keystone. You're safe."

His voice was gentle as he spoke. He'd seen panic attacks before, and the woman was definitely verging on one. Bodie wanted to do everything possible to avoid it.

Standing this close, he could now hear her heart beating fast. Her breaths coming and going in short, quick succession.

There were too many people. He needed to get her out of here. Away from the crowd and somewhere quiet.

Wrapping an arm around her waist, Bodie gently tugged her toward the break room. He didn't give a damn if people were watching or not. His sole focus was the woman at his side.

Once they entered the room, Bodie closed the door and guided her to the couch. Her body was unnaturally rigid. Her breathing ragged. As he crouched in front of her, he studied her face, but it was almost like she wasn't seeing him. Like he wasn't there at all.

Slowly, Bodie touched his hand to her cheek. Even though he'd kept the touch soft, she startled at the contact.

"Hey there, darlin', you with me?"

She didn't respond. She wasn't with him. Not yet.

Leaning closer, Bodie lowered his voice to a whisper. "Breathe with me."

Taking a deep breath in, he held it for three seconds before slowly releasing it. Then he repeated. Again and again.

At first, Maya watched him. Her eyes moving from his mouth to his rising and falling chest. It took three breaths before she joined him. Three breaths before they were breathing together in unison. Her eyes had lifted and were boring into his. Watching him like he was her lifeline.

"That's it, sweetheart."

They continued like that for minutes. Bodie didn't care how long it took. Hell, he'd sit here all night if that's what it took.

Relief filtered through his chest when her heart rate began to slow and light re-entered her eyes. Her skin was still pale, but it no longer bordered on stark white. Bodie waited another two breaths before rising to sit beside her. He moved his hand to her back, rubbing slow, firm circles over her shirt. "Are you okay?"

She nodded, but remained silent. Even though he wanted to hear her voice, it was a hell of a lot better than the complete lack of response he'd received minutes ago.

"What happened?"

He wasn't sure he'd get an answer. Even if he did, he was almost certain it wouldn't be the truth.

"I...I thought I..." She swallowed before shaking her head. "I'm sorry."

"You don't need to say sorry. What scared you out there?"

She blinked once. Twice. Clearly desperate to hold back the tears. Her eyes darted around the room like she was looking for words.

Then she surprised him.

"I used to work as a lab technician. One night, while I was on shift, my workplace was broken into and robbed. It was...traumatizing...to say the least. I've been having flashbacks."

He looked down to see she held her hands together tightly in her lap. Her knuckles were white. He moved his free hand over both of hers. "I'm sorry that happened to you, Maya. It must have been terrifying."

He wasn't just sorry. He was angry as hell. Angry that the people he and his team were trying to bring down were still hurting others. Murdering innocents.

Maya looked at Bodie's hand. She didn't try to pull hers away.

"I watched colleagues die. Friends. People I'd known and worked with for years. I thought *I* was going to die. I was *supposed* to die."

Those last words made a shard of pain shoot through Bodie's insides.

"Maya, look at me." Her gaze slowly rose to his. "You are alive because you are supposed to be alive. You had a close call with death, and I'm unbelievably sorry about that, but don't for a minute think you shouldn't be here."

Tears gathered in her eyes. This time, she didn't try to stop them. "I spend half my days being scared, and the other half feeling guilty for being alive."

A tear fell down her cheek. Then another. They were silent tears. As silent as she clearly tried to keep her pain.

Bodie had never hated Hylar and his men more than he did at that moment. The assholes should never have touched Maya's life.

He gathered her close and held her tightly against him. Tears soaked into his shirt. The wetness the only sign that she still cried. The woman in his arms wasn't fragile. She was strong and brave and a survivor. But that didn't mean she had to do it all alone.

Bodie wanted to fight for her. Fight *with* her. To protect her not just from Hylar, but from all the evil in this world.

He held her until she pulled away. She quickly wiped her face.

"What triggered you tonight, Maya?"

"I thought I heard something. But I'm pretty sure it was just in my head."

Bodie was trained to detect a lie. A person's heart rate changed. Their pupils dilated and they often looked away. Sometimes they even touched their face or fidgeted.

Maya did none of those things. But she also told him very little. "Something" was vague. He wished she'd be more open. Maybe it was time to tell Maya the truth about who he was. Not tonight, but when she was in a better state of mind.

A level of trust had been developed. Hopefully, enough for him to tell her his truths, and for Maya to share hers without running.

She turned her head to look at him and studied his face. "Thank you, Bodie. For pulling me in here and letting me cry all over you."

She leaned forward and pressed a kiss to his cheek. Heat burned from the place she'd pressed her lips, penetrating right down to his chest.

Maya stood. Her face was slightly redder than usual, but other than that, no one would think she'd been crying. "We should get back out there."

Bodie stood. But instead of walking straight out, he took a step closer to her. "Are you sure you're okay?"

"I'm okay. Thank you again."

"You're safe with me, sweetheart." *Always.*

For the rest of her shift, Maya moved on autopilot. She ignored the unease, pushed down the lingering fear, and worked.

She made more mistakes than she cared to remember. A heck of a lot more than usual. But no one kicked up a fuss about a single one of them.

Maya felt Bodie's eyes on her the entire time. They tracked her movement, almost like he was waiting for her to have another freak-out.

She wouldn't. As it was, she wanted to dig her head into the ground and pretend he'd never seen her like that…weak.

Christ, she was a mess. She'd fallen apart over something that existed in her head.

She tried to focus on the positive. That Bodie *had* been there. That he'd saved her from having what would likely have been a full-blown panic attack right in the middle of the bar.

Even though she felt embarrassed that she'd cried into his shirt, she also felt like a small weight had been lifted off her chest...because someone in Keystone knew something about her terror.

Maya thought she'd seen some anger in his features, but she wasn't entirely sure. The man was good at masking his emotions.

As the last customer exited, Maya finally breathed a sigh of relief. She'd survived the shift. Now she could go home and curl up into a ball under her sheets. She had been scheduled to do post-close cleanup with Trish, but her boss had already replaced her with Shayna.

Maya felt so much relief that she could go home earlier that she didn't have the capacity to feel guilty or embarrassed.

Grabbing her phone from the back room, Maya said a quick goodbye to the women before stepping outside. That's where she found Bodie, leaning against the wall of the building, looking all kinds of perfect.

Her eyes flicked from the street back to him. "Hey."

He'd left over five minutes ago. At least, she'd *thought* he left.

"Hey. Ready to walk home?"

And now he was walking her home. It was like his appeal knew no bounds.

"You don't have to. I mean, I'm okay."

He took a step forward. "I know."

Bodie reached down and threaded his long, warm fingers through hers. His large hand engulfed her smaller one, making her feel feminine and safe.

Maya was so distracted by the feeling that it took her a few minutes of walking before she found her voice. "You're holding my hand again."

Okay, if she was trying to come across as simple, she'd hit the nail on the head with that comment. But it was taking her muddled brain a moment to catch up.

"I am. Is that okay?"

Seeing as his touch was sending waves of heat up her arm and through her body, she'd say it was. "Yes."

A smile spread across his face. Maya's insides turned to mush, and all thoughts of what had happened—or almost happened—that night fled. His touch made her feel protected. Something that had been in short supply recently.

"What was your second choice?" Bodie asked, breaking into Maya's thoughts.

"Second choice?"

He lifted a shoulder. "Well, you came to Keystone for the ice skating. If you couldn't have come here, which town would have been your second choice?"

"Carmel, California." The truth popped out before she could think of a different answer.

Bodie nodded. "I've never been there but heard good things."

"I haven't been either, but whenever I researched it, there were pictures of the ocean and it looked…peaceful."

He nudged her shoulder with his. "Regret choosing Keystone?"

"Oh, not for a second. I'm really enjoying it here." There was so much truth to that. The job, the relationships she was building…there were moments where she almost forget what she was doing here. "What about you? Enjoying Keystone?"

"Yeah, Keystone's growing on me," Bodie said. "It's not as average as I thought it would be."

It was certainly more than average to Maya. It was her sanctuary. "What do you like about it?"

"For starters, the food is awesome. Those burgers we had the other night were epic. And I already know where I want to take you next. The Thai place on Third Avenue. I got takeout the other night and I kid you not, it was the best Thai I've ever had."

Where he wants to take her next? The man was already planning their second date. Not that she was entirely sure it *was* a date. Friends kissed on the cheek…but they didn't usually hold hands.

If she had a bit more courage, she might ask him.

"Aside from the food, the people are also nice here. Trish. Shayna. Roe," Bodie continued.

"They're all great. Especially Roe." Just the mention of him made a smile pull at her lips.

"He is. He made a point to talk to me the moment I was hired. Well, less a talk than an interrogation. I think I may have passed."

Maya laughed. "I think he likes you."

"Good. I also think he has a thing for Trish."

"Really?" Maybe that was why the guy was at the bar every night. "I'm not great at reading people, so I didn't pick that up. It would explain a lot though."

"You're probably better than you think."

Doubtful. But she was intrigued by his comment. "What makes you say that?"

"You knew I was an awesome person when we first met."

She'd been so overwhelmed by the broken glasses and the new job, she hadn't paid him nearly enough attention. "I definitely knew you were a kind person," Maya said. "When I broke those glasses, no one else even attempted to help me. I'm pretty sure I heard the table of guys at the back snickering."

She caught Bodie's scowl. "They were assholes."

That was a given. "Can I ask you a question?"

His hand tightened around hers. "Ask me anything."

"Were you in the military?"

There was the slightest pause before he answered. "Yes."

So Shayna was right.

"Does that bother you?" he asked.

"No." It actually made her feel a bit safer. He wouldn't win a fight against the men who'd broken into the lab, but he might stand more of a chance than the average person, depending on his training. "Thank you for your service."

He dipped his head.

Any person who could give years of their life to serve their country deserved a heck of a lot of respect and gratitude in Maya's eyes.

When they arrived at her house, she finally untangled their fingers. Her hand felt cold without Bodie's touch. "Thank you for walking me home."

"Thank you for letting me."

Pulling her keys from her pocket, Maya unlocked the door. She was about to step inside when she stopped. Turning back to Bodie, she blurted the question that had been playing on repeat in her mind during the walk. "Do you like me?"

The slightest frown marred his brows. "Yes."

"Like-like...or friend-like."

One side of his mouth drew up. "What does 'like-like' entail?"

"Dates. Holding hands." Maya hesitated on the last one. "Kissing."

"I definitely like-like you."

"But last night, you didn't...kiss me."

Oh boy. Had she really just said that? She sounded like some desperate woman, pouting over not being kissed.

"Would you like me to kiss you, Maya?"

Would she? It was safer if he didn't and they remained friends. A kiss would change things. Deepen things...and then she'd leave.

"Do you *want* to kiss me?"

If he said no, she'd walk inside and close the door. She would not be sad. She would not bring up kisses again.

"Yes."

Yes.

Yes, he wanted to kiss her.

It took everything in Maya not to react to his word. Not to melt to the floor or suck in a million tiny breaths.

One of his hands snaked around her waist, pulling her body against his, while the other touched her cheek.

Slowly, Bodie dipped his head. She didn't take her gaze from his. She couldn't. She was transfixed.

Then his lips touched hers, and her eyes shuttered. A slow hum began to vibrate in her veins. His lips were gentle, yet they ignited a heat that swept through her limbs.

Raising her hands, Maya swept her fingers through his soft locks. The last bit of space between them was eliminated when he tightened his hold on her waist.

His lips moved, sweeping across her mouth. His tongue eased inside, touching hers. It was a kiss that had every one of Maya's nerves on edge. She was surrounded by the guy. And it wasn't enough.

As if hearing her thoughts, Bodie lifted her body, her legs instinctively wrapping around his waist. He turned and pressed her back against the wall beside her door. His kiss changed subtly. His lips pressing a touch harder, his tongue massaging hers.

Suddenly, Maya wanted to give this man everything. She wanted him to take from her, as she took from him.

That thought sent a shot of fear through her veins.

She couldn't fall for this guy. She couldn't fall for anyone. Love and happily ever afters didn't play a role in her life. All she would do was get hurt.

Placing her hand on his chest, Maya gave a small push. Bodie immediately lifted his head. She took a moment to calm herself. Her breathing was labored. Embarrassingly so. Whereas he seemed completely fine.

It took a long moment for either of them to speak. She was too weak to ask him to let her go just yet. Being held by Bodie was the closest to peace she'd ever felt.

Eventually, she slid down his body, willing her arms not to pull him back.

"Thanks again for walking me home, Bodie."

His eyes remained heated. "Lock the door after me, darlin'."

Then, just like he'd done the night before, he pressed a kiss to her cheek. But this time, it didn't feel like a kiss from a friend.

Maya quickly moved inside the house, knowing that whatever had just transpired between them wasn't something that would be easy to walk away from.

CHAPTER 11

*B*odie knocked on Maya's door.

The memory of last night's kiss was still fresh in his mind. The feel of her body wrapped around his...it damn near lit a fire in his veins that was impossible to extinguish.

Light shuffling sounded from inside the house, then he heard a small gasp from the other side of the door. He swallowed a chuckle, assuming she'd just seen him through the peephole.

The door slowly crept open, stopping partway. He saw only half of Maya. The other half remained behind the wood. It was still enough to have his jaw dropping.

Maya wore a towel. Water droplets slid down her chest while her wet hair flowed over her shoulders.

"What are you doing here?"

Right now, he was just trying to control his burning libido.

He ran a hand through his hair, using every ounce of self-control he possessed to keep his mind off the fact that she was likely naked under that towel.

"Can I tell you after you get dressed?" *So I don't do something that will have you running hard and fast from me.* "I can wait out here if you like?"

Maya looked down, almost like she'd forgotten she was only wearing a towel. There was no way Bodie would have missed it.

"Oh. Sorry. Yes, I need to get dressed. Come in and wait in the living room. I don't want you freezing."

Bodie barely felt the cold at the best of times. Right now, he was as far from cold as it got. Stepping inside, he closed the door after him. He didn't bother stepping over the thread. He didn't want Maya to know that he'd noticed. It might disturb her perception of its ability to create safety.

Maya moved to the bedroom while Bodie stood in the living room. He waited until he heard the click of the door closing before breathing out a pained breath.

Christ, the woman just about undid him. She tested every shred of self-restraint he had.

Walking over to the couch, he put down the jacket he'd brought before casting his gaze around the room. This was his second time inside, and he still hated that she lived here. The place smelled of dampness and mold, and paint was peeling off the walls. If it hadn't been for Bodie, the house wouldn't even have adequate heating.

The landlord had to be a real asshole to rent it out in its current condition. Probably why he'd let a single woman with no identification live there. Because no one else would want it.

The only thing that made Bodie feel better was the knowledge that Maya wouldn't be here for long. Not if he got what he wanted.

His attention shifted as Maya walked out of the bedroom. She wore a white turtleneck sweater and tight blue jeans that showed off her toned, athletic legs.

"You look amazing." There was no way he could keep that thought to himself.

A rosy-pink color tinged her cheeks. "It's just a sweater and jeans."

Bodie had a feeling the woman looked stunning in anything.

"It just so happens that both of us have late shifts today. I was hoping you were free to spend the day with me."

He heard the slight increase in her heart rate. He only just suppressed the smile that threatened to pull at his lips.

"I am...free, that is."

Good.

Lifting the jacket, he handed it to Maya.

Her brow furrowed. "What's this?"

"An old snow jacket of mine. Doesn't fit me anymore, so I'd like you to have it."

That wasn't entirely true. He'd actually purchased it a few days ago just for her. He'd intentionally bought a large one to validate his story.

Maya was already shaking her head. "I can't take your jacket."

Bodie stepped forward and pressed it into her hands. "If you don't take the jacket, we'll both miss out on today's fun." There was no way he was taking her out in the snow without a warm jacket. Where he only required a sweater, Maya needed a hell of a lot more.

Her gaze dropped to his lips for a moment. He itched to lower his head. Touch his lips to hers.

"What's today?" she asked, eyes returning to his.

Raising a finger, he trailed it along her cheekbone, loving the way she subtly pressed her face closer to his touch. "It's the first day of snow. I was hoping you'd take a gondola lift to the top of Keystone Mountain with me. We can watch the snowfall together."

There was a flash of excitement on her face before she tried to mask it. She didn't do a very good job. Bodie liked that. It meant he could trust what he saw.

"You want to go on a gondola ride with me? To watch the snow?"

"I do. Absolutely." He didn't know why the woman was

surprised. He thought he'd made his feelings abundantly clear last night.

Maya's tongue slipped out to wet her bottom lip. This time it was Bodie staring at *her* mouth. "I'd love to."

She'd barely gotten her words out when his self-restraint snapped. He dipped his head, pressing his lips to hers. Maya moaned deep in her throat and leaned into his body.

This kiss wasn't the same as last night. It wasn't slow and exploratory. It was deep and intense. Christ, she tasted good. Tasted. Felt. Everything about the woman was amazing.

Bodie moved his hand from her cheek to her neck. Maya's hands pressed to his chest before gliding down, causing him to harden to an unbearable degree.

Bodie kissed her like a desperate man. Like he would never get enough of her…which he probably wouldn't.

Seconds passed…then minutes. Eventually, he knew that he needed to end it. If he didn't, he'd be doing a lot more than kissing her.

Lifting his head, he felt the resistance from Maya. "You test my self-control like no one ever has before."

Maya opened her eyes to stare up at him. They were glazed over with lust. "Why does kissing you feel so right?"

Who the hell knew, but Bodie felt it as well. "It feels right to me, too."

For a moment, Maya didn't speak. Then, slowly, she untangled herself from him.

Bending down, Bodie lifted the jacket, which had fallen to the ground. "Do you need anything else before we go?"

Maya looked like she wanted to say something. If the woman said "him," then all bets were off. He'd be taking her right there and then.

"No. I'm ready to go."

Squashing the disappointment, Bodie smiled and headed for the door. It was better this way. He wanted to tell Maya the truth before they got any deeper. The truth about who he was and why he was in Keystone.

~

GOOD LORD, they were high up.

Maya had never been on a gondola lift before. If she was completely honest with herself, it was a bit terrifying. Especially sitting beside a man who had to weigh over two hundred pounds.

Was it possible their combined weights would snap the cable?

"Relax." Bodie whispered the word in her ear. It sent a tingle down her spine.

"You're sure this is safe?"

"I would go so far as to argue that it's safer up here than on the ground."

She gave him a skeptical look. "How is that?"

He lifted a shoulder. "No chance of disappearing under a layer of snow."

Maya laughed. "Okay, but if this thing breaks, it's going to send us straight into the snow anyway." And it would be ten times harder to get out because they'd probably have broken limbs.

Why did her mind always take her to worst-case scenario?

"Focus on the snow that's falling around us."

It *was* pretty magnificent. Small, fluffy snowflakes fell from the sky in a steady stream. The grass on the ground had been covered quickly.

"Have you been on a gondola lift before?" she asked.

"I have. When I was in high school, we went on a ski trip. It was awesome."

She couldn't imagine teenage Bodie. In her mind, he was and always had been six and a half feet of muscle, and all man.

"Did you enjoy school?"

His smile grew wide and was nothing but genuine. "Loved it.

School meant football, and football was my entire life as a teenager. I was even offered scholarships at a few colleges to play once I graduated."

That wasn't a surprise to her. The man looked like he would excel at any physical endeavor. "Which college did you choose?"

"None."

None? Why would anyone turn down a scholarship?

As if hearing her thoughts, Bodie began to explain. "This is going to sound sappy, but I felt like there was something more out there for me."

"That doesn't sound sappy. It sounds like something didn't feel right and you trusted your gut."

Bodie reached for her hand and threaded his fingers through hers. Even though they were both wearing gloves, she could still feel an influx of warmth transfer from his hand.

"That's exactly how it was." He studied her face. "What about you? Did you always know what you wanted to do?"

It was more like Maya knew how to *survive*. She didn't have parents who had saved a college fund for her, just like she didn't have a family to live with while she figured things out.

"I didn't have a lot of options. I was good at science. Tutoring during high school allowed me to earn some money. I was lucky that a couple of colleges offered me full scholarships." She shrugged. "I was *very* lucky."

She repeated those words because she often needed to remind herself of the fact. A lot of people who grew up in foster care weren't lucky at all.

Bodie's expression sobered. "It sounds more like hard work than luck. I'm sorry your childhood wasn't great."

It wasn't. The feeling of being unsafe had unfortunately been her reality in more than a few homes. The constant, though, no matter which home she went to, was the lack of love and connection.

"I never knew any different. I don't remember my parents. Foster families treated me well enough." Most of them.

Bodie shook his head. "You deserved more than 'well enough.' You deserved consistency of care. Love."

Maya swallowed hard. She'd given up on that dream a long time ago. "We don't choose the life we're born into. We just do the best we can with the one we're given."

Growing up, she'd, of course, realized that her life was different than those of her peers. There were many times she'd craved what others had. It had taken her years to come to terms with the fact she never would.

Bodie scrubbed his free hand over his face, like he was in pain. "I want to tell you something. Something important."

A sliver of fear crept down her spine at his words. Was it something bad? Wasn't that how all bad admissions began? Swallowing, she nodded. "Okay, but before you do, I need to admit something to you first. Something that you probably already know, but if I say it out loud, then you don't need to wonder."

His expression didn't change. "You can tell me anything."

She didn't quite feel like she could tell him "anything." But she wanted to tell him this.

"I'm not completely okay right now." *Understatement of the century.* "Most days I feel like I'm on the edge of an iceberg, waiting for the ground to melt beneath my feet. Or for waves to push me into the icy ocean."

She felt Bodie's hand tighten on hers.

"I feel...fragile."

Like the smallest thing can break me.

When he remained silent, Maya hurried to continue. "So, what I'm trying to say is, everything kind of scares me to death right now...including my feelings for you."

Love wasn't familiar to her. Love had never been a part of her past. She'd literally been running for her life for months, and everything about the idea of falling for someone scared the crap out of her.

Bodie remained silent for another beat before he spoke. "I understand, Maya. You can't handle any big curveballs in your life right now. Thank you for being honest and open with me."

As she studied his face, she realized that something had changed from a minute ago. His features had become a little more closed off. "I'm sorry, maybe I shouldn't have told you that."

He shook his head. "Like I said earlier, you can tell me anything."

"What was it you wanted to tell me?"

He hesitated. Almost as if he was trying to decide on his next words. "That I'm grateful to have met you."

Maya was almost certain that those were *not* the words he'd been intending to say.

He lowered his head a fraction. "I'm really glad you shared that with me. If you ever need to share anything else, I'm a great listener."

Maya was tempted. So damn tempted. But if she told him her whole truth, she would be doing nothing but putting him in danger. It would be entirely selfish on her part.

She forced a smile. "Thank you."

Dipping his head, Bodie kissed her. But it wasn't the same kiss as that morning. No, that kiss had been without hesitation. All lust and desire. This one was riddled with insecurities. Unspoken secrets.

CHAPTER 12

*M*aya shot into a sitting position. The nightmare was still fresh in her mind, toying with her sense of reality.

He'd found her. Here in Keystone. He'd been standing in her doorway watching her. Waiting to take her. His face had been in the shadows, but when he spoke, she knew it was him.

Maya scrubbed her hands over her face. God, when was it going to end? The running, the fear...

Shaking her head, she darted her gaze around her dark bedroom. Her dark, *cold* bedroom.

Moving her hands to her arms, she rubbed them to ward off the chill. Holy crap, it was freezing. Felt-like-she-was-out-in-the-snow kind of freezing.

Argh, had her heating stopped working again? It would be just her luck.

Reluctantly, Maya threw back the sheets. There was no way she was getting back to sleep now. She was fully awake in the igloo-like room she was sleeping in.

Climbing out of bed, Maya gasped when her feet touched the

cool floorboards. She didn't need to see the wall heater in the living room to know it was off.

Flicking the light switch, she frowned when nothing happened. She tried twice more and each time, the room remained in a cloak of darkness.

Goose bumps rose over Maya's skin that had nothing to do with the cold.

Grabbing her phone from the bedside table, she turned the flashlight on before moving into the living room. She tried the next light switch. Again, absolutely nothing.

A shiver coursed down her spine as a cool breeze brushed over her skin.

Where the heck was that coming from?

Maya moved through the kitchen to the back door, stopping after only a few feet.

The door was open. Not completely open, but enough to let the outside cold in.

Almost involuntarily, Maya took a small step back. Had she left it open? The door was old and often got stuck. She'd gone out the back just before bedtime to bring the potted plants in, so it was possible that it was her...

No. She was always extremely careful. Overly so.

Glancing around the house, she took a moment to listen for any small noises. There were none.

She'd taken a single step forward when shuffling sounded from outside.

Her heart lurched in her chest.

She had a gun. She'd bought it just before arriving in Keystone. She needed to go get it. But that required her legs to move.

Maya forced one foot toward the bedroom. Then another. Before she knew it, she was running to the bedside table and digging beneath socks in the middle drawer to grab the weapon.

If the bastard had found her, her best shot at survival was to aim and shoot.

Her legs threatened to cave beneath her as she stepped into the backyard. She held the flashlight in one hand and the gun in the other. The gun felt heavy. She'd taken a few shooting lessons in the towns she'd lived in before Keystone, but she was far from confident.

And this was different from shooting in a range. So very different.

Maya shined the light around the yard, waiting for a figure to jump out at her. Her bare feet sank into the snow, freezing her skin.

When no one appeared, Maya took a moment to calm herself. Maybe they'd left. That didn't make sense to her, and she had no idea why someone would open her back door to simply leave, but as far as she could tell, no one was here.

Her fingers were icy cold. She was standing in the snow wearing nothing but a sleep top and pants. Her teeth began to chatter.

Okay. She needed to get inside before she froze to death.

Lowering the gun to her side, Maya was just turning back to the house when something jumped in front of her.

Her scream pierced the quiet night as she fell backward into the snow. Because she held her phone and the gun, she wasn't able to brace herself and fell hard on her backside.

Cold filtered through her clothes to her skin. She ignored it as best she could as she lifted the light to see a cat running through her yard.

She pressed a hand to her chest as she pushed to her feet and went back inside.

The moment the door was shut, she dialed Bodie's number. Unlike last time she'd called him, tonight there was no hesitation. The power was out; she was thoroughly freezing, and someone had opened her back door.

"Maya? Are you okay?"

She'd expected him to sound sleepy. After all, she was waking him up in the middle of the night. But he sounded wide awake. In fact, she almost thought she heard the sound of the wind in the background.

"I'm really sorry to call so late..." She tensed her jaw to stop her teeth from chattering.

"What's wrong?"

"The heating stopped working again. Actually, I think all the power is off."

And I went outside and fell in the cold, wet snow and now may be getting hypothermia.

"I'll be there in two minutes. Put on the snow jacket while you wait."

Bodie had already hung up. Relief rushed through her system. Thank god for him.

The shake in her limbs intensified, causing the gun to almost slip from her fingers.

Crap. The gun. Bodie had said he'd be here in two minutes... she couldn't let him see her holding this.

Rushing to the bedroom, Maya shoved the weapon back into the middle drawer, covering it with her socks. The shake in her fingers made the task almost impossible. Maybe the hot water was working. At least she could run her fingers under it and bring some feeling back into them.

Maya moved to the bathroom sink and turned on the tap. She waited for the water to heat. Instead, it remained icy cold, furthering her own chill.

Fantastic.

Turning the water off, she hung her head for a moment, trying not to feel sorry for herself. She wasn't sure if Bodie planned to look over her electricity or just take her to his place. It had taken him over an hour to fix things last time.

A knock sounded on the door, causing Maya to sag in relief.

When she opened it, she was greeted with a very unhappy-looking Bodie. An unhappy and disheveled-looking Bodie. His hair was windswept, like he'd just been running, and his pants were visibly wet from the snow.

Had he run from his apartment?

"You look frozen. Where's the snow jacket?" There was an edge of danger to his voice.

"I was going to run my hands under hot water first but it didn't work." She paused as another shiver ran down her spine. Her clothes were damp and the breeze from outside was almost unbearable. "You go-ot here quick."

At her stutter, his jaw visibly tensed before he moved inside. Without responding, Bodie pulled Maya into his chest. When his big, warm arms wrapped around her, Maya sank into him, enjoying the way he surrounded her like a giant heater.

She wanted to absorb as much of him as possible.

His arms stiffened. "You're wet."

It was a statement, not a question.

"The back door was open. I checked outside and fell in the snow."

She expected him to ask about how the back door came to be open. He didn't.

Maya pulled back, immediately feeling the loss of the warmth. Looking up, she saw the intense look on Bodie's face hadn't diminished. In fact, it was relatively icy.

"It's late, I'll take you back to my place. I'll wait here while you change and pack an overnight bag."

Maya didn't argue. In fact, she wanted to breathe a sigh of relief at the fact she wouldn't be staying here the rest of the night.

Disappearing into the bedroom, she threw on some dry clothes, then packed a small bag. The new clothes didn't seem to improve the chill in her body. It was like the cold had seeped into her bones. Iced her limbs to an unbearable degree.

When she stepped out, Bodie was waiting for her, holding the snow jacket open. She stepped straight into it. The jacket was warm, but it didn't hold a candle to the warmth of Bodie's body from moments ago.

Maya watched as he moved to the back door. Opening it, he scanned the yard. He remained there for a beat before firmly closing and locking the door.

When he turned back to her, for the first time that night, there was a small smile on his lips. The smile seemed...wrong, though, and appeared entirely forced. "Let's get out of here. I left the car on so it's nice and warm."

Warm sounded divine.

Bodie took the bag from her fingers before leading her outside to his car.

She would love to know what the man was thinking. She was almost certain he was attempting to shield her from his thoughts.

Why?

Before she could ask, another shiver wracked her body. Holy cow, she was so cold that even the snow jacket wasn't helping.

The trip to Bodie's house was quick. The car heating was powerful, and some feeling began to filter into her fingers. She still couldn't quite shake the chill though. And she'd begun to feel a dull ache in her chest.

Stepping into Bodie's second-floor apartment, she was greeted with a small, but modern space. It was the complete opposite of the old house she was renting. Instead of peeling paint and a cold interior, his apartment was shiny, warm, and new. There wasn't an old thing in sight.

Bodie took her hands in both of his, drawing her attention. "You're still freezing." He just about growled the words.

"I'm okay."

If anything, that comment made his features harden further. It was probably the rattle of teeth that did it.

"Why don't you have a shower and I'll make you a hot drink?"

There wasn't a single thing she could think of that sounded better. "Are you sure? It's pretty late."

Or early, depending which way you looked at it.

"Yes. Spare bedroom is through the door to your left and there's an adjoining bathroom."

Maya was about to turn when she hesitated. She wrapped her arms around Bodie and hugged him. She hugged him tightly, digging her head into his chest.

"Thank you." The two words left her mouth barely louder than a whisper.

For a moment, she felt his lips press into her hair. She sunk deeper.

Eventually, she pulled away and moved across the room, stepping into the bedroom. The place was luxurious. Or maybe she'd just gotten so used to living in rundown accommodations that she was no longer used to clean and modern.

When she stepped under the stream of warm water, she let out of a long sigh. The heat was pure bliss.

Maya felt better for about a minute. Then she started to feel worse. Not worse as in cold, although she still wasn't warm, worse as in lightheaded. Maybe it was the quick change in body temperature. Or maybe it was the exhaustion from the nightmare and being woken.

Placing her hands on the shower wall, Maya breathed through the dizziness. It didn't go away.

Reluctantly, she switched off the shower. Sit. She needed to sit…before she fell.

Stepping out of the shower, she'd just wrapped a towel around her chest when the room began to spin. She made a grab for the towel rack but missed, hitting the tiled floor with a thud. She was vaguely aware of pain to her hip, which took the brunt of the impact.

A second later, she heard the bathroom door opening. She felt Bodie's hand on her cheek.

She was pretty sure she'd locked the bathroom door. It hadn't kept the man out. Maybe there was nothing that would.

BODIE LIKED to think he was pretty good at keeping a lid on his emotions. Right now, he was only just containing his fury.

Maya's silent alarm had woken him twenty minutes ago. Luckily, he'd been in his car, watching the house. It was something he'd been doing regularly. He hadn't slept in his own bed in days and only allowed himself a couple hours of sleep a night.

Her street was generally pretty packed with parked cars. That, in combination with his tinted windows, meant he never raised suspicion.

The moment the alarm beeped, Bodie had sprinted to the back door. The asshole heard him coming and took off before he could grab him.

Bodie had chased him down the street. That's where he'd stopped. He hadn't been prepared to leave Maya unprotected. For all he knew, the guy's friends could be close behind.

If he hadn't installed that alarm...He sucked in a deep breath, not even wanting to think about that.

Bodie filled his kettle with water. Maya being in his house brought him a small level of comfort. He needed her safe. Not just because it was his mission to do so, but because there was a connection between them. A connection that made Bodie want more than friendship.

Yet, he couldn't help but feel that he'd failed her tonight.

Just as he placed a tea bag in the cup, he heard the shower turn off. He went still as her heart skipped a beat.

Looking up, he watched the closed bedroom door. That's when he heard the thud of her body hitting the floor.

Bodie took off toward the bathroom. He didn't think to slow his speed. She needed him, so he was going to be there.

At the sight of her lying helplessly on her side, fear gripped him. The only small reprieve was that she was breathing. He crouched by her side and placed a hand to her cheek. Still cold. "What happened? Are you okay?"

Her eyes snapped open, and she tried to push up into a sitting position, but her arms shook with the effort.

Taking hold of her arms, Bodie helped pull her up. He didn't remove his hands once she was sitting.

"It may have been the quick change in temperature...or my heart."

Bodie ground his teeth at the uncertainty in her voice.

Wrapping his arms around her back and legs, he lifted her and walked to the adjoining bedroom. Placing her on the bed, he quickly moved back to his room to grab one of his shirts.

"Lift your arms." He tugged the shirt over her body and the towel. "I'll be right back."

Bodie grabbed her hot tea from the kitchen counter before returning to the bedroom. Maya was exactly where he'd left her.

"Drink this, then you need rest." He was being bossy and wasn't sure if he should expect an argument, but he didn't get one. Instead, she gingerly took the cup and drank from it slowly. There was still a slight shake in her hands, which Bodie hated.

When she was done, he took the cup with the intention of leaving her to get some sleep.

"Bodie..." Her voice halted him before he took a step. "Will you lie with me? I can't seem to shake the cold. And you're warm."

Having her in his arms was exactly what he wanted. "Give me a sec to turn everything off and I'll be right back."

The relief on her face made his heart swell. His woman needed him, and he'd be damned if he wasn't going to be there for her.

Bodie went to his room and quickly changed into a T-shirt

and shorts before turning everything off. He usually slept in a lot less, but he wanted Maya to be comfortable.

When he returned to the bedroom, Maya was already under the sheets, curled into a ball.

Sliding in beside her, Bodie snaked an arm around her waist and pulled her body against his. Her cold feet touched his legs, her cold hands on his arms.

"I know I say this a lot," Maya whispered. "But thank you."

Bodie didn't want to be thanked. He wanted Maya to be safe. In his mind, she was already his. That made her his to protect.

"Thank you for trusting me enough to let me help."

A few minutes later, Maya's breaths evened out. He didn't fall asleep so easily. He was too busy thinking about the man he'd chased tonight.

The man who was just like him.

CHAPTER 13

*M*aya woke the same way she'd fallen asleep. Cocooned in Bodie's heat. His front remained pressed to her back, and the weight of his arm was heavy against her side.

But where last night, her whole focus had been on the warmth and comfort he emitted, this morning, it was in a far different place. This morning, she focused on the way his arm touched the underside of her breasts. On the firmness of his chest along her back. The way his breath brushed against her neck in the most delicious way.

The longer Maya lay there, silent and unmoving, the more aware—more sensitive—she became to their intimate embrace.

When his thumb moved against her skin, Maya's stomach muscles tightened.

Oh, lord, grant her strength. Strength to not do something stupid like press her butt tighter against his crotch, even though every part of her wanted to.

She should roll away from him. She wasn't in Keystone to find love. She was here to stay hidden.

Almost like he knew she was considering getting up, Bodie tightened his arm around her middle. "Mm. I like waking up like this."

His voice was deep and rough around the edges. His lips so close to her neck, she almost felt each word he spoke. Goose bumps skittered across her skin.

Like her body had a mind of its own, it nuzzled further into him. "You feel good."

And strong and warm and like you fit around me in the most perfect way.

A soft growl vibrated from his chest to her back. "Can't possibly be as good as you feel."

Hm, she wasn't so sure.

When his fingers began to draw light circles on her ribs, she used every effort not to move a muscle. There was the light barrier of clothing between his hand and her flesh, but she swore she felt his touch like they were skin to skin.

Move away, Maya. Get up.

But her body refused to listen. Refused to give up the amazing feelings his touch evoked.

Bodie's head lowered to her neck, and Maya's breath caught. The touch was soft but searing. She felt it right down to her toes.

His lips began to feather kisses across her skin, each one as light as the next.

She tipped her head to the side, exposing more skin. Wanting more kisses. Wanting more *him*. He took advantage, touching the newly exposed skin with his lips.

Maya rolled onto her back and Bodie hovered over her, his weight pressed firmly into her side. A soft purr escaped her throat. She sounded like a stranger.

His head rose, and for a moment, she wanted to pull it back to her body. But then he looked at her. And a million things were communicated without a single word being said.

Tenderness. Desire. Passion. Hell, the man looked at her like she belonged to him. Like they belonged together.

Her heart stuttered in her chest.

Maybe we do...belong together.

The whisper came to Maya softly. Allowing her to believe for a moment that maybe this could actually work. She could find happiness with another, despite her circumstances.

Bodie raised his hand and moved a lock of hair from her face. "I could easily become addicted to you."

She wet her lips. His gaze immediately zoned in on her mouth. "I think it's too late for me. I'm already addicted." Madly, hopelessly addicted.

His eyes darkened until they were almost black.

She wanted him to kiss her. She wanted it so badly, she was afraid of what might happen if he didn't.

He placed his hand over her heart, just above her breast. "How are you feeling this morning?"

"Fine." Well, not exactly fine, but that had nothing to do with her heart issues. "I'm usually okay after a good night's sleep." And last night had definitely been a good sleep.

When Bodie remained still, Maya decided she was done waiting. Lifting her hand, she pulled his head down and pressed his lips to hers.

Desire pooled in her core. It was heaven.

As their mouths melded together in perfect harmony, Bodie shifted so that his weight hovered fully over her, his arms bracketing her body.

Maya glided her fingers through his hair. So soft.

When his tongue slid between her lips, she couldn't stop the moan from escaping her throat. Tasting him did nothing to dull her need for the man. It made her crave him more.

She was acutely aware that she was naked beneath the shirt. That every inch the material slid up, was another inch of skin exposed.

When his hand slid below the shirt and touched her bare thigh, a small shudder raced up her spine. He held it there for a moment, almost like he was waiting to see if she pulled away.

Maya lifted a leg and wrapped it around his waist. She pulled him to her, obliterating any space between them.

His hand continued to glide up her thigh, her hip. When he reached her ribs, her breath caught. Her heart was thudding so hard, she was sure he could feel it. He was so close to her breast. A mere inch away. She wanted to groan out loud in frustration that he didn't close that distance.

"Are you sure this is okay?"

Yes. Yes, yes, and yes.

"This is okay, Bodie. I'm okay. Kiss me."

Bodie's lips returned to hers, but his hand didn't continue to her breast.

Instead of waiting, Maya placed a hand over his larger one and moved it that final inch. The ecstasy that coursed through her when his long fingers enclosed her breast was like nothing else. It had her spine arching. Her chest pushing higher.

When his hand began to move—massaging and stroking—a sharp ache built in her core. The fire inside her raged, burning her up.

Bodie took his lips from hers, trailing kisses down her cheek. Then he was pushing up the other side of the shirt, taking her other breast with his mouth.

A strangled cry escaped her lips. Her body jolted wildly.

He sucked and tugged on her nipple while his other hand continued to play.

More…she wanted more.

Maya wrapped her other leg around his waist, pressing and rubbing her core against him. As much as she tried to dull the ache between her thighs, it was impossible.

Bodie switched breasts, taking the other nipple into his mouth.

"Bodie…" His name was a tortured cry from her lips.

His hand moved from her breast to the apex between her thighs. His fingers touching her. Moving across her sensitive clit.

Maya squirmed beneath him as he moved in circular motions, switching between touching her softly and firmly. The pressure in her core built.

Bodie came off her nipple and trailed kisses back up her chest to her neck. She threw her head back as he sucked. As his thumb continued to move on her clit, he inserted a finger inside her.

Maya's body jerked in awareness. She tried to pull him closer, farther inside her, but it was impossible. He pressed her body to the bed. Not giving her an inch of wiggle room.

Desire throbbed inside her in the most intoxicating way.

"What do you want, Maya?"

She'd stopped wanting a long time ago. All she felt now was need. "You."

The single word was all she said. She wanted him inside her. Their bodies connected in the most intimate way.

Bodie stood—and Maya thought she might cry. He pressed a kiss to her temple before disappearing out of the room. He was back within seconds, condom in hand.

Bodie stripped off his clothes and stood bare in front of her. His eyes remained on hers, intense and heated. He looked at her like he was claiming her as his own.

He quickly sheathed himself. Then he returned to her. His delectable weight once again hovering over her body. He made quick work of pulling his shirt over her head. Then they lay there, skin to skin.

She felt him at her entrance. It made the throbbing inside her intensify.

Fire laced her veins as he entered her slowly.

Once he was seated completely inside her, he trailed a gentle finger down her cheek. "I thought they were making it up. The connection and desire. They weren't. I just hadn't found it yet."

Maya felt it too. It was so strong, it almost scared her.

Before she could overthink it, Bodie dipped his head and kissed her. The kiss was long and sweet, and it lingered as he began to move. He pulled out of her slowly and thrust back in at an even pace.

Maya dug her nails into his shoulders and threw her head back. The pleasure was overwhelming. So powerful, it consumed her mind and body.

Bodie took her hand, threading his fingers through hers before raising them over her head. Dipping down, he kissed her again, but this time firmly. Hard and thorough.

His thrusts sped up. He moved deeper. Faster. Her breasts bounced, her sensitive nipples brushing against his chest.

When Maya felt the touch of his thumb at her core, her body shook, and a cry escaped her lips.

"Fucking flawless."

He whispered the words under his breath. His powerful thrusts continued. He was relentless. Every inch of her body was being stimulated. She was teetering on the edge of a cliff, so close to tipping off.

Bodie's head lowered, and he nipped her ear. That's what pushed her over.

Maya cried out as her body spasmed around him. She moaning in untamed pleasure as the orgasm all but destroyed her.

Bodie continued to pump into her, his breathing shifting. Becoming more erratic.

A low growl erupted in his chest, and his body tightened before he came. She felt him throb inside her, his whole body tense.

Perfect. The man above her was perfect. Perfect and powerful and fierce.

Her feelings for him were so strong. Feelings she hadn't known could exist so deeply and so quickly.

Bodie nuzzled his face into her neck. His left hand still entangled with hers.

There was a slight ache in her chest. She wasn't sure if it was the defect or had more to do with the man above her.

There wasn't a single thing that felt wrong about them, about what they'd done.

And that terrified her.

WHAT BODIE and Maya had experienced wasn't normal. It was so much more. He felt more certain about that than he'd ever felt about anything.

The woman touched a place inside him that no one had ever touched before. She made his heart race and his world silence.

Five of his seven teammates and brothers had found their person. They were changed men. Better men who had new reasons to live.

Bodie had seen the changes in his friends. He'd known he wanted that. He wanted the unexplainable connection. The person to live for. To *breathe* for.

It was Maya.

Bodie carried his laptop to the dining room table. Maya had just entered the bathroom and he could hear her moving around in there. He initiated a video chat with his team. He doubted all of them would answer. It was rare that all were free at any given time.

Wyatt, Asher, Kye, and Oliver immediately came onto the screen. At the sight of his friends, a smile pulled at his lips. "Hey. How are you guys?"

"We're great. I think the real question is, how are you and Maya?" Asher asked.

"We're good." Better than good, but he didn't need his friends knowing that just yet.

Oliver was shaking his head like he already knew.

"Any updates?" Wyatt asked.

The smile slipped from Bodie's lips. "Someone was at her house last night. They tampered with her electricity and would have entered her home if I hadn't been there." Luckily, the security system he'd installed didn't rely on electricity.

Oliver cursed. "Did you catch him?"

"No. I was in my car when the alarm alerted me to the breach. I caught sight of the guy inside her kitchen, but he heard me coming. Took off. I didn't catch him."

Kye frowned. "Damn."

Bodie could think of a much stronger word. "I plan to check her place over today. I'm also going to try to convince her to stay with me for a bit."

After what they'd just experienced together, he was hoping it wouldn't be too hard to talk her into it. Hell, he'd probably be asking even if there wasn't danger.

Wyatt nodded. "Good call."

"Anything new on Project Arma?" Bodie asked, not sure what kind of answer he wanted to hear.

The looks on his friends' faces gave Bodie his answer before anyone spoke.

"Not a peep from them," Wyatt said. "Everyone's been checking on family members regularly, and so far, nothing. Nothing to report from Marble Falls either."

That was good news. The only downside of it was, that meant Hylar and his men were still hidden and out of reach...for the moment.

"Let me know if I can be of any help," Bodie said, knowing his whole team was frustrated by the situation.

"You *are* being a help," Wyatt responded immediately. "The guilt's been eating at Quinn. Guilt that she didn't drag Maya here when she first met her. That she didn't help her more. If you can protect Maya, you'll be helping Quinn."

Bodie nodded. He understood why Quinn might feel that way, but it wasn't her fault that Maya had run.

"She'll be safe. I won't be letting anything happen to her."

Not a chance.

"Okay. I see what's happening here. You've already claimed the woman." Oliver chuckled. "Soon it's just going to be me and Cage left."

The mood immediately lightened. Kye shrugged. "Doesn't bother me. I plan to be a lone wolf forever."

Bodie wanted to laugh at the guy. If he met his woman, he would have no choice in the matter.

He was running out of time before Maya finished getting ready, but he had one more thing he wanted to mention to his friends before they hung up. "I'm going to tell her."

Asher leaned back, blowing out a long breath. "Big call, Red. How do you think she'll take it?"

He hoped she'd be receptive. Prayed she wouldn't get scared and run.

"Hopefully well. If not…" Bodie actually had no idea what he'd do. "Hopefully well," he repeated.

He'd been about to tell her the other day on the gondola, but then she'd spoken to him about being fragile. About standing on the edge of an iceberg, waiting for the ground to melt beneath her feet. And he just…hadn't been able to. Instead, he'd wanted to keep things light.

But now it was time.

"I like her," he continued to his friends. "A lot. I don't want there to be secrets between us. I don't want to skulk in the shadows to protect her anymore. Maybe if I'm honest with her, she'll be open and honest with me."

Open up to him about any details she might have left out when talking to Quinn. And maybe then, the team could build on what they already had.

Oliver nodded. "Good luck."

"And remember," Wyatt added. "You need support out there, you let us know."

"Will do." Hopefully, it wouldn't come to that.

CHAPTER 14

*T*wo hours. That's how long Maya had to wait until her shift finished and she was back in Bodie's apartment, cocooned in his arms.

It was two hours too long.

No matter how many people filled the bar, no matter how busy she got, she felt him. The gentle touch of his hand on her shoulder as he passed. The light brush of his front against her back when he reached for something above her.

Every so often, he stopped and whispered something sweet into her ear. She could barely even remember what he said each time. But she could remember what he made her *feel*.

Hot and bothered.

Over the course of the day, she'd somehow rationalized in her head that it would be okay to enjoy her time with Bodie until she had to leave.

It would still be safer for her to keep him at a distance, of course it would. She knew what they shared wasn't going to be a lifelong relationship. One, because she would be leaving town soon enough, and two, because she was pretty sure she was incapable of giving and receiving love.

Neither of those were things she was going to dwell on at the moment. For now, she was going to enjoy the rare peace she felt. Affection was so foreign to her that she couldn't help but want to feel it for just a bit longer. Hang on to the happiness that had been so fleeting in her life.

Leaving him would hurt...but he would be a memory that she would cherish. A memory that she would be able to call on in the hard times, and remind her that she had been cared for once.

Maya grabbed a case of beer from storage and headed back to the bar. She'd only taken a few steps when Bodie was there, taking the heavy crate from her struggling hands.

"I got it," he assured, his voice deep and rumbly.

He didn't walk forward...and it took Maya a moment to realize he wanted her to go first. Her cheeks flushed as she took hurried steps toward the bar. She didn't miss Bodie's light chuckle from behind.

It was absurd that she was flushing at all after what they'd done that morning. After spending the entire day together.

Bodie had gone back to her place with her to see if he could fix the electricity and hot water.

When he hadn't been able to, he'd admitted that it looked like something a professional needed to handle. Maya had done some quick calculations in her head. Calculations of what an electrician and plumber might cost her. How much that would set her back. It all added up to the usual—too expensive. But it was too cold to go without heating.

She'd been on the verge of a full-blown anxiety attack when Bodie offered for her to stay with him. He'd even added that she could stay as long as she liked.

The relief had hit her hard. So hard, she'd almost thrown herself at the man as a sign of her gratitude. She'd only just contained herself.

Mentally shaking her head, Maya returned to the bar and

served the next customer. She'd just grabbed another glass when Shayna popped up beside her.

The other woman leaned close. "I need the goss. You and Bodie are on a whole new level of eye-fucking tonight. You screwed him, didn't you?"

Maya's face heated at Shayna's crass words. After working together for a few weeks, Maya had thought she was used to her up-front nature. Clearly not.

"I don't really want to talk about it right—"

"Aha!" Maya jolted at Shayna's exclamation, spilling the whiskey she was pouring onto the bar. "You are! Otherwise, you would have said no."

Grabbing a cloth, Maya wiped the spill. She had basically no experience talking to women like Shayna, so she scrambled for how to respond.

"It's busy. We should really be working." And by *we*, Maya meant Shayna should really be working.

At that moment, Trish walked past, pausing behind them. "Maya's right. Get back to work, Shayna."

Shayna rolled her eyes but kept the smile on her face. She had been working at the bar for years and knew that it would take a lot for her to actually get in trouble.

Well, Maya hadn't been working there for years, so didn't want to push her luck.

Turning back to the counter, Maya finished the drink and handed it to the woman on the other side before holding out the EFTPOS machine.

Shayna leaned into her again, this time speaking softly. "I think it's awesome. I do. Just…be careful. There's something about the way he looks at you…"

A frown marred Maya's brow as she pulled the machine back and looked up at the other woman. "How does he look at me?"

"Like he's ready to fight the world to protect you."

Um, well, that didn't sound so bad.

"It's intense," Shayna continued. "Especially considering how short of a time you two have known each other."

Maya's eyes shot across the room, searching for him. Bodie was collecting glasses from a table. But unlike when she'd seen him in the hall, this time he didn't look so relaxed. He looked edgy. Almost worried.

Shaking her head, she smiled back at Shayna. "Thank you, but I'm okay. I appreciate your concern." She truly did. It was nice when *anyone* was concerned for her.

Shayna nodded before getting back to work.

Time passed a little faster after that. Maya moved from customer to customer, serving everything from bottles of beer to fancy cocktails. Every time she mixed a drink, she gave herself a mental pat on the back. She was getting the hang of this bartending stuff.

She tried to keep her mind off what Shayna had said, she honestly did, but the other woman's words kept creeping back into her thoughts.

It's intense.

Wasn't intense a good thing? Surely, someone wanting to fight the world to protect you was good. God knew, she could use a little protection.

She wondered what people saw on *her* face when she looked at the man. Desire. Yearning. Desperation…

Blah. She certainly hoped not.

As it neared the end of the night, the crowd began to thin out. Finally. She was exhausted. The disturbance in her sleep the previous night had really wiped her.

Moving to a table, she piled the glasses onto her tray. She'd just turned and taken a step when her hip bumped the corner of the table, which in turn caused the tray in her hands to wobble.

As the glasses slid off, Maya scrunched her eyes shut and waited to hear them shatter.

The sound never came. Not even a clatter.

Opening her eyes, she scanned the floor. No broken glass. But there were shoes. Bodie's shoes.

Looking up, she saw Bodie holding two glasses in his hands. One side of his mouth lifted. "Got them."

God, he must have been close to have caught them. And he must have lightning reflexes. "Thank you. Should I add this to the long list of times you've saved me?"

He placed the glasses on the table before reaching his hand out and pushing some of her hair behind her ear. It took a great deal of effort for her to not lean into the touch.

"Only if I can add this to the long list of times I've been unable to refrain from touching you."

The man could touch her whenever he wanted. "Deal."

And then you can touch me again. Run your thumb over my cheekbone. Press your hand to my waist.

Not that she necessarily needed his touch. He just had to look at her for her hormones to go into a frenzy.

"Good. Because the list is long. And I predict it will get longer."

The guy had all the words. If they weren't standing in the middle of a public space, she had no doubt he would be kissing her. Or she would be kissing him. Either way, their mouths would be touching.

Wetting her lips, she glanced to the side. That's when she spotted them. Two men in police uniforms walking up to the bar.

Her heart lurched into her throat. Then it began to pound hard.

Were they here for her? Had he sent them?

The tray in her hands suddenly felt heavy. So heavy it began to wobble again. She was sure she would have dropped it had Bodie not taken it from her unsteady fingers. Thank god he did. The attention from the loud noise would have given her away.

The two men were waiting at the bar. Were they waiting to

speak to Trish? Waiting to ask about a Maya Harper? Runaway witness?

When one of the officers turned his head, Maya shrank back, angling her body behind Bodie's larger form. He didn't say anything, probably too confused and wondering what the heck she was doing.

She couldn't explain it to him. She didn't dare tell him she was a wanted woman and there was a chance the officers were here to take her away. To take her to *him*.

Maya eyed the hallway that led to the back room. Could she make it there without being seen? Were there enough people left in the bar to block her from view?

Maybe. Or maybe it would expose her.

When Trish began talking to the officers, Maya used the moment of distraction to move. She mumbled something to Bodie about needing to go out back. She'd barely whispered the words, so there was a strong chance he hadn't heard.

Then she moved. Fast enough to get out of sight quickly, but not fast enough to draw unwanted attention.

∾

BODIE SAW the change in Maya's body language immediately. One moment, she was calm and happy. Maybe even a little flustered by his touch.

The next, she was stiff as a board. Shrinking back in what looked to be fear.

He followed her gaze to see her staring at two uniformed officers. She stared at them like they were enemies.

He sensed her desire to run before she took her first step.

Bodie readied himself. He would protect her. Stand between her and anyone who would try to hurt her, even if it was someone with a badge.

The two officers waited at the bar. They didn't appear tense or ready for action. Nothing about their body language alerted him to them being on the chase.

When the tray began to shake in Maya's hands, he gently took it from her fingers and placed it on the table.

Maya inched behind him, fear all over her face.

When Trish approached the officers, Maya mumbled that she was heading out back before quickly disappearing. He was tempted to go after her. He would. But first, he wanted to see what the police wanted. Were they after Maya like she clearly believed?

Bodie walked behind the bar but remained a few feet away. He tried to look busy as he listened to what they said. It only took a few seconds to establish that they weren't here for her. They weren't here for anyone. The officers had finished their shift and were stopping for a drink on the way home.

Running a hand through his hair, Bodie turned toward the hall. The first place he checked was the break room, where staff kept their belongings.

No Maya. Then he checked the storage room. Still nothing.

As he neared the end of the hall, he listened at the staff bathroom door. First, he heard her heartbeat. Then her breaths, coming hard and fast.

When Bodie knocked, her breath hitched.

"Maya, it's Bodie. Are you okay?"

His words were greeted with silence. It stretched to the point where he wondered if she was going to answer at all. His worry intensified.

He was moments from breaking the lock when her quiet voice sounded. "I'm okay. I'll be out in a sec."

"Okay. But if the reason you're back here has anything to do with the officers out front," *or everything*, "I heard Trish speak to them and they're just here for a beer...nothing else."

More silence. It stretched a good twenty seconds before the click of the lock unlatching sounded and the door opened.

She looked more nervous than scared now.

He took a step forward. "Are you sure you're okay?"

"I'm sure."

She nibbled her bottom lip. She looked small and vulnerable. All Bodie wanted to do was tug her into his arms and make her feel safe.

Maya stepped around Bodie and out of the bathroom.

He wanted to know why the police had caused such a strong reaction. Why they'd made her run. Why her entire body had frozen in fear. Now wasn't the time to push.

Tomorrow, he planned to tell her *his* truth. *His* reason for being in Keystone. Then, maybe, she would tell him hers.

CHAPTER 15

*M*aya trailed a finger down the heavy arm lying across her waist. Bodie's heavy arm.

She'd been awake for at least five minutes but hadn't moved a muscle. She didn't need to move. This was where she felt most at peace.

After they'd left the bar last night, Maya had been quiet. She hadn't known what to say because anything that even began to explain her reaction to the police officers involved a whole lot of confessions.

Thankfully, Bodie had filled the silence with his chatter. In fact, he'd acted like nothing had happened. As if she hadn't run to the bathroom and hidden from police like a wanted felon.

Sooner or later, Bodie would want to know the truth. She just had to hold off telling him until it was time to leave.

At the thought of leaving him, pain shot through her chest. Maya ignored it. She was going to enjoy their moments together while she had them.

She hadn't looked at a clock, but if the sun poking through the cracks of the blinds was any indicator, it had to be about midmorning. Plus, she felt well rested. Something that she'd rarely, if ever, felt upon waking in the last few months.

Rolling onto her other side, she looked straight at Bodie. Surprisingly, his eyes were wide open.

"You're awake?"

Well, *obviously*. He'd just been so still that she'd assumed he was asleep.

The corners of his lips pulled up. "I am."

Bodie's hair was lightly ruffled, and he had the beginnings of a morning beard. The man was beautiful, in a wild warrior kind of way.

She was all too aware of the hand that gripped her hip. Of the leg that brushed against hers.

She ran a finger across his muscular shoulder. "What should we do before work today?"

She knew what *she* wanted to do. And it didn't involve taking a single step outside this room.

A small frown marred his brow before he cleared his features. "I thought we could have breakfast together." He paused for a moment before continuing. Suddenly, Maya got an uneasy feeling in her gut. "After breakfast, there's something I'd like to discuss."

Something he'd like to discuss...as in, something important. Or upsetting. Something that couldn't be discussed casually in bed.

Trepidation crept down her spine. "Sounds serious."

Was he going to demand a reason for her actions last night? The very idea had her brain scrambling for what she'd say.

He gently squeezed her hip. "It's nothing to worry about, just something I've been needing to tell you."

If that was supposed to make her feel better, it didn't.

Before Maya could respond, his head dipped, and his lips pressed to hers. "Mm, how do you taste so good this early?"

She smiled, but the smile didn't come quite as easily as it

might have moments ago. "I probably have morning breath." She definitely had morning breath. "I shouldn't even be letting you kiss me."

He kissed her again. "Nope. No morning breath. You taste amazing."

Her gaze flicked to the connecting bathroom. "Is it okay if I shower before breakfast?" That should give her just enough time to completely freak out over what Bodie might have to tell her.

He nuzzled his head into her neck. Some of the tension in her chest eased. "Only if there's room for two in there."

Two as in—

Before Maya could finish that thought, Bodie jumped out of bed and lifted her into his arms.

"Bodie!"

She tried to be angry, but couldn't stop the laugh as he marched them to the shower. All other thoughts leaving her mind.

An hour and a half later and they were finally sitting down to breakfast. They'd remained in the shower for quite a while. Certainly a lot longer than it would have taken had they showered separately.

The thought brought heat to Maya's cheeks.

"What are you thinking about over there?"

Maya's gaze shot across the table to Bodie. Damn. The man was too observant. Either that, or she was too obvious. Probably a bit of both. "That we have quite a feast this morning."

The feast part was true. Together, they'd whipped up eggs, bacon, bagels...they'd even gone to the effort of roasting some vegetables. Well, Bodie had gone to the effort. Maya had been more an assistant in the kitchen.

Bodie gave her a knowing smile. The man knew what she'd said had *not* been what she'd been thinking, but he didn't seem willing to call her on it. Thank god. "I learned a long time ago that breakfast is the most important meal of the day. If you don't start with the right food, you may as well stay in bed."

Maya chuckled. If that were true, she shouldn't have gotten out of bed for months.

She took a bite of her egg and bacon bagel. Bodie was eating his open with a knife and fork. Much classier. "And bacon is the right food to start the day with?"

"A hundred percent it is." Bodie shoved a huge fork full of food into his mouth. It made Maya laugh again. "Bacon and bagels for the taste, and eggs and veg for the nutrition."

"I would argue that eggs can be eaten for the taste too."

She actually loved eggs. Not that she'd eaten a whole lot of them lately…not since money had been an issue.

He lifted a shoulder. "I can take them or leave them. My mom used to make them every single day when I was a kid. Let's just say I got over them."

At the mention of his family, Maya paused. "How's your family doing with you living in Keystone and them being in Jacksonville?" She couldn't imagine that the distance would be easy.

"I haven't lived in the same state as them for a while. Not since enlisting. Everyone's pretty used to it."

She was about to ask him how often he spoke to them when he got a question in first.

"What about you? Keep in contact with any of your foster families?"

Not one. But she chewed her food slowly, considering her words. "Some kids in the foster system find people they really click with. A family that becomes their family. I never found that."

Sometimes, she'd thought she was close. Then she'd realize it was just wishful thinking.

"I'm sorry."

She kept her eyes on her food. "It happens. The positive is that I have no strings. I can pick up and leave town quickly without letting anyone know. I don't have to worry about whether anyone needs me."

Or worry that their lives could be endangered because of me.

"Have you had any long-term boyfriends?"

Okay. Now he really was going to think she was pathetic. "No. Not long-term. I dated a couple of guys in college, but nothing ever stuck." In other words, she'd never had anyone in her life for an extended period of time. Every single person, every relationship, had been temporary.

Just like Bodie.

She barely stopped herself from rubbing her hand over her heart at that thought.

"Well, my family will love you."

Her head snapped up. "Your family?"

He shoved another piece of bacon into his mouth and nodded. "Yeah, wait until you meet them all. My straight-laced brother. My neurotic sister. And don't get me started on my overbearing parents. They'll drag you into their home and never let you leave."

Some of the hard casing around Maya's heart softened. The guy planned for her to meet his family? That had to mean that he saw them as more than a short fling.

Mentally shaking her head, she crashed back down to reality with a thud.

She would never meet them. She couldn't plan a future with Bodie. She couldn't plan a future with anyone. Hell, the guy didn't even know her real last name, for goodness' sake!

Bodie shoved more food into his mouth. His plate was already nearly empty. "Although, we're going to have to work on your cooking."

Maya frowned. "My cooking?"

He shrugged. "I saw the way you flipped those eggs. Your technique could use a little refining."

Was he serious? "Maybe I was just mimicking your bacon-flipping technique."

He put a hand to his heart. She couldn't help but laugh at the wounded expression on his face. "I am an awesome food flipper, thank you."

She lifted her bagel to her lips. "Guess I'm not too bad then, either."

For the remainder of the meal, the conversation was light. Bodie teased Maya about her cooking, her supposed sleep talking —which she was pretty sure didn't exist—and her refusal to eat the bagel with a knife and fork. Maya gave it all right back to him.

By the time their plates were bare, her cheeks hurt from smiling so much. They tidied quickly before Bodie took Maya's hand and led her to the couch.

That's when the energy in the room shifted. The playfulness of moments ago disappeared, and visible tension entered Bodie's body. Maya suddenly remembered his earlier mention of the conversation they needed to have.

Crap. It had all but slipped her mind.

Swallowing the dread that was already crawling up her throat, Maya sat beside him on the couch and wrung her hands in her lap.

"I've tried to wait as long as possible to tell you this. I wanted us to build trust first."

This was sounding more and more like an introduction to something she *did not* want to hear.

"I'm telling you now because I think you know me. You know that you can trust me. That I would never hurt you."

Maya nodded. That was true. She did trust him not to hurt her. But she also knew that trust was fragile. It could be there one second and lost the next.

"I told you that I was in the military. I was a Navy SEAL. A few years ago, my commander signed my team up for a program called Project Arma. We received specialized training and drugs to help with our physical performance and recovery time." Pain flashed briefly over Bodie's face. "But the program was a front for something else. We didn't know until it was too late."

Numbness began to creep into Maya's limbs. Like she knew where this was going but didn't want to believe it. "What was it a front for?"

For a moment, Bodie appeared apprehensive. It was the first time she'd seen an ounce of fear on him—and she just knew whatever he was about to say was going to change everything.

"The drugs they injected into us…made us stronger and faster than ordinary people. I don't feel the cold as much as I should. I heal quickly."

Maya's heart sped up. Her breaths moved in and out of her chest in quick succession.

"I can see through darkness. I hear things I shouldn't be able to hear."

"Like a person's heartbeat…" Her voice was barely a whisper.

"Like a person's heartbeat."

Maya shot to her feet and took a hurried step back.

He was just like *them*. Like the men who had murdered her colleagues! Snapped their necks. Thrown her into the wall.

Bodie stood too, slowly, raising both hands in front of him. "Remember, Maya, you *know* me. You know I'd never hurt you."

"How did you find me?" Because now that she knew he was like them, there was no way he was here by coincidence.

"Quinn."

Maya's eyes widened. "Quinn, as in the reporter Quinn? The woman who worked for *The New York Times*, who I met in Tyler?"

Bodie nodded. "Quinn is the sister of one of my teammates, and the partner of another. She told us about you. About your connection to people like us. She wanted to come, but unfortunately couldn't make it. I came here to help you."

Help her? He didn't even *know* her.

"Why would you want to help me?"

"Quinn and Wyatt went to your apartment in Tyler to find you, but you weren't there. She's worried about you. Because your enemies are *our* enemies, and we don't want to see you get hurt."

Enemies...so Bodie wasn't aligned with the men who broke into the lab? "Those people who robbed the lab, the men who killed my friends...they're your enemies?"

"Yes." This time, his expression hardened. His features darkened. "My old commander, a man named Hylar, is their leader. We've torn down most of their organization but he's still out there, with a few men at his side."

Maya's heart was racing. So much so that she almost felt faint.

"So this," she pointed to him and then herself, "this is you getting close to me to protect me?" A sharp pain stabbed at her chest.

He took a step forward. She took another step back.

"No. The plan was to befriend you before opening up about the truth. I wanted you to feel safe first. Everything else that has developed between us happened naturally."

Maya didn't know what to think. The man in front of her was like *them*. Not one of them, but like them. Those men who were so evil, so powerful, they belonged in fictional stories.

But she hadn't met Bodie by accident. He'd searched her out. Found her. Gotten close to her. All with an ulterior motive.

If Bodie had found her, surely that meant *he* could find her.

Thick panic seized her whole body. "How did you find me?"

"We tracked the location from where you sent the last email to Quinn."

Okay. That was good. Only his team knew about that email, then, and no one else should be able to track her here.

Bodie stepped forward again. When she didn't step back, he reached out and touched her arm. "I'm sorry to dump all of this on you. I know you may need some time to get your head around it."

Time...she felt like she needed an eternity.

"The other night, when I called you because the heating wasn't working, your clothes were damp from the snow and your hair was windswept." It wasn't a question...but it was.

Bodie scrubbed a hand over his face. "When I got to town, I set up silent alarms and cameras at the exterior entrance points of your home so that whenever someone came or went, I was alerted."

He'd been watching her home with *cameras*?

"Just the exterior of the home," Bodie repeated firmly. "That night, I was sitting in my car on the street when the back door alarm went off. I caught a guy in your kitchen. I chased him but didn't catch him."

Ice pooled in her veins.

They'd found her.

She'd thought she was hidden. She wasn't. Not even close. Bodie had found her...and now someone else had, too.

Thoughts raced through her head. Of running. Of slipping away in the dead of night. But now that Bodie had found her—now that *he'd* found her—it was too late.

She chafed her arms, trying to ward off the cold. "I'm just... I'm struggling with the fact that you've been watching me and I didn't know." She avoided eye contact, finding it difficult to look him in the face. "I'm trying to wrap my head around the fact that you're like *them*. I'm feeling sick to my stomach at the fact that there was someone who broke into my home."

A million different feelings rushed through her, and she didn't know how to cope with a single one of them.

A part of her whispered that she should be happy Bodie was there to look after her. But the Bodie who stood in front of her felt different from the man he'd been ten minutes ago.

Maya wanted to ask about the future. About how he intended

to keep her safe. Did he want her to return to wherever the rest of his team was? What did he plan to do about their relationship?

She didn't ask any of that.

"I need to grab some things from my place before my shift starts."

When she finally looked up at him, she saw the hurt on his face. The hurt and maybe a bit of fear, too. He didn't even try to hide it.

"Of course. I'll drive you."

Maya nodded, feeling somewhat numb. She had been careless in emailing Quinn to say she was okay. In sending that email, she'd lost her illusion of safety.

CHAPTER 16

*M*aya was driving Bodie crazy.

It had been three days of her barely uttering a word to him. Of quick nods in the hall. Short conversations that he initiated...

The woman was still living with him, but in his guest room. With the potential danger, there was no way she could go back to her own place. Not to mention the house was ridiculously cold.

Living with her, and not having her, was hell.

"What did you do, son?"

Bodie dragged his gaze from Maya to Roe, who sat on a stool across the bar. Roe's eyes were narrowed at Bodie in accusation.

"Would you be believe me if I said nothing?"

Roe scoffed. "Not for a second. You two are usually disgustingly obsessed with each other and terrible at hiding it. For the last few nights, she's barely spared you a glance."

The old man was right, and it was eating Bodie up. He missed having her eyes on him. "You're very observant."

Roe took a sip of his beer. "I was the chief of police for twenty years. You don't get there by letting things escape your notice."

Bodie knew all about the other man's past. Wyatt had done a

thorough background check on everyone at Inwood Bar, Roe included. Even if Bodie didn't have that information, he probably would have picked out Roe's employment history on his own. It was obvious he saw more than most. Probably more than most wanted him to.

"Let's say I did screw up." Not that he had. He'd just run out of time. Their relationship had progressed quickly, and he hadn't wanted there to be secrets between them. "How would you fix it?"

Roe leaned back in his seat, a thoughtful expression on his face. "Without knowing what you did, it's hard to say. But I will tell you that women are complex creatures. Sometimes they require gentleness. Other times, a more direct approach. The trick is knowing which one *she* needs."

Immediately, Bodie's eyes swung across the room, back to Maya. The bar wasn't busy tonight, so it wasn't hard to find her. She was wiping down tables. Strands of her golden-brown hair had broken free and were falling over her cheeks.

The only time he ever felt short of breath was when his eyes landed on her. His feet itched to go to her even now.

"You'd think she'd be more inclined to the gentle approach," Roe continued. "But my gut tells me it's the opposite."

Direct. That's basically what he'd already done. What got him into this mess. "And if I get it wrong?"

"You're screwed."

If it wasn't so true, Bodie would have laughed. "How did you get so wise?"

A knowing smile came over Roe's face. "See these lines around my eyes? That's wisdom. You get it from years of making mistakes, then picking yourself back up and learning from them."

"I've got a few of those lines myself. But I don't know that I have a lick of wisdom in me."

"Your skin is crystal clear, boy. You got a lot of mistakes yet to make."

This time Bodie did throw his head back and laugh. The man was right about one thing; he had many mistakes yet to make.

He heard Trish coming his way before he saw her.

"Bodie, are you able to do the close tonight with Maya? My damn cat got out. Neighbor has a fit whenever it happens. Thinks Kerny's going to eat his precious chickens."

Bodie kept a straight face. He sure wished *his* biggest problem was a cat escaping. "Not a problem, Trish."

"Good. And do me a favor, make the woman smile. She's been moping around the place for days and it's bumming me out. The customers are going to get so depressed, they'll stop coming."

Roe grunted his agreement from across the bar.

Bodie tried not to flinch. Everyone could see it. She was miserable. Miserable because of what she'd learned about *him*.

He nodded. He would do his best. But when he didn't know what the hell the woman was thinking, it felt near impossible.

Moving down the bar, Bodie served the next customer, still lost in thought.

He'd hoped that once he told her the truth, she'd be shocked, but quickly get used to the idea. She'd lean on him for support and allow him to protect her. He'd also wanted her to talk to him about the break-in and any missing details she might not have told Quinn.

That certainly hadn't happened. Would it change after a few days? A few weeks?

Bodie didn't have weeks. He needed to get back to Marble Falls. They were still fighting a war against Hylar and his program.

One thing Bodie regretted was sleeping with her before telling her the truth. He almost cringed at his own poor judgment. Well, less poor judgment and more low self-restraint. But there was no part of him that had slept with her just to get closer. Even the thought had his stomach clenching in revulsion.

Bodie had told her as much, but he wasn't sure if she

completely believed him. He also knew that her bubble of safety had been popped. She'd thought she was safely hidden. His being here told her that she was findable.

He started making the next customer a drink, his mind never far from Maya.

From everything she'd told him, it seemed that she wasn't used to being cared for. She'd gone through life alone, without anyone to stand by her side. Allowing someone in, allowing someone to know you, wasn't always automatic or easy.

He had no idea how the families who'd cared for her hadn't fallen in love with her on the spot. She was caring, smart, empathic...and the fact that she'd turned out the way she had, after facing such adversity in life, showed how damn strong she was.

Bodie was just holding the EFTPOS machine out to a customer when he noticed Maya slipping out of the room. Her brow was furrowed and her lips pressed together. She didn't look okay.

MAYA NEEDED AIR. She felt like she was suffocating.

There weren't even that many people in the bar tonight, yet it felt crowded. The need to get out was clawing up her neck.

Walking down the hall, she headed toward the staff room before remembering Shayna was on break. She continued to the storage room instead and closed the door firmly behind her. The moment she was alone, she let the quiet steady her. It wasn't silent. Far from it. The sound of people and music still snuck into the room. But it was nowhere near as loud as out there.

She sucked in some deep breaths, blowing each one out slowly.

It had been three days since Bodie had told her his truth. That he'd tracked her down. Put surveillance cameras on the exit points of her home. He'd even admitted to placing a tracking device on her phone.

She almost wanted to cry, she felt so stupid. Stupid for thinking she could stay out of sight. That she could just stop in a town, get a job and no one would find her.

Stupid in thinking that Bodie, this amazing man, just *happened* to walk into her life. God, for the first time ever, she'd actually thought that someone might want her...she should have known better.

Embarrassment heated her cheeks. She was an obligation to him. No matter which way you spun it, that's what Bodie's presence in her life boiled down to.

Maya didn't have many options though. He was her best chance of staying alive. She had to trust him to protect her. If anyone could, it was him.

She wouldn't be leaving him once she had enough money. He wanted her to go to Marble Falls with him. Meet his friends. The idea was almost scarier than a man chasing her across the country, wanting her dead.

What happened once his obligation to protect her ended? Once her feelings had deepened?

Everything in her life thus far had taught her that people leave. No matter how much you want them to stay, no matter how much faith you have in them, they leave.

Every family she'd ever been placed with had seen her as temporary. Her whole life had been a carousel of rotating homes. Foster parents that never lasted. Siblings she'd grown to like, then had to leave behind. Hell, even friendships had been short-lived.

At every turn, her main life lesson had been that relationships are impermanent. The only person she could truly rely on was herself.

What if she fell in love with the guy...and he left?

Trusting him felt scary. Actually, no, trusting him felt absolutely terrifying.

Disappearing felt safe.

Shaking her head, Maya turned toward the door just as the one behind her opened. The one that led to the street behind the bar and was used for deliveries. A man stepped inside—but he was no deliveryman. There was a smile on his lips. A smile that in no way reached his eyes. One side of his face was yellow with what looked to be old bruising.

He looked familiar, but she couldn't quite figure out where she'd seen him before.

"Remember me, sweetheart? You were having some fun on my lap before that boyfriend of yours interrupted us the other night?"

Recognition hit hard. He was the drunk guy from the bar. The man Bodie had thrown out when he'd grabbed her. She took a small step back. "Bodie told you not to come back."

She actually wasn't sure exactly *what* Bodie had told the man, but she was almost certain it was something like that.

The man tilted his head. Even though he was nowhere near as big as Bodie, he still looked a whole lot more capable than her. "You think I'd actually listen to the asshole?"

"I need to get back."

Before he could respond, three more men stepped through the same open door. The three who had been with the guy that night.

Fear stabbed at her chest and rendered her motionless. "Wh-what do you guys want?" She only just got the words out, icy terror now freezing her insides.

Maya inched toward the door. Before she could anticipate his actions, the man in front leaped forward, grabbing her arm. "Your boy punched me right in the face. Then he almost choked me to death."

Maya's gaze flicked down. Sure enough, she saw the bruises

that remained on his neck. "I don't see how that has to do with me—"

"Oh, it has everything to do with you. What better way to get payback than to mess with his woman—the bitch he clearly wants no other man to touch—while he's in the very next room?" The man tightened his grip on her arm, causing her to whimper in pain. "We're going to have some fun…and piss that asshole off."

His friends moved forward, causing Maya's stomach to cramp in alarm.

She opened her mouth to scream, but before she could utter a sound, the door behind her flew open, slamming against the wall. In the next moment, Bodie was by her side.

She almost flinched when she saw the expression on his face. Deadly rage. He was almost unrecognizable.

This time, Bodie didn't ask the man to remove his hand. He reached out and grabbed it. The fingers around her arm immediately released as the man howled in pain.

Bodie stepped in front of Maya, pulling her behind him. "I told you not to come back." He still didn't release the man's wrist. The guy was almost crying. "I don't like people disobeying direct orders. And I certainly don't like people touching my woman."

One of the other three stepped forward. "Get your hand off him!"

Maya took a hurried step back, hitting the door behind her. A large part of her wanted to run out of the room, but she couldn't tear her eyes off Bodie and the scene in front of her.

Were these men really so stupid as to pick a fight with someone Bodie's size?

Almost in unison, the three men lunged.

Maya gasped as violence broke out around her. One of the men threw a punch, while another kicked out. One even attempted to head butt Bodie.

He deflected each attack easily, even as he threw a punch. A loud crunch echoed through the room. A man fell to the ground like a sack of potatoes.

Bodie aimed for the next guy. The same thing.

"You come anywhere near her again…and I'll kill you." Bodie said the words with such quiet fury, the men went still.

Then the two men still standing took off toward the back door. Bodie didn't chase after them. Instead, he stood watching while the injured men peeled themselves off the floor before following them out.

Maya remained where she was, the room suddenly feeling silent and empty. She didn't know how long she stood like that.

Bodie closed both doors before moving toward her. His eyes remained hard for a moment before they finally gentled. "Are you okay?"

He stood so close, she could feel warmth radiating off his body. "I'm okay. I…they didn't do anything."

Reaching out, his fingers grazed her arm. The exact spot where the man had grabbed her. She looked down to see that her skin was already bruising.

Bodie cursed under his breath. "I'm sorry he touched you."

"I'm really okay, Bodie."

It had frightened her. Of course it had. And she didn't want to think about what would have happened had Bodie not entered the room when he had. But she'd been through worse. She'd seen worse.

He watched her for another beat before pulling her into his chest and wrapped his arms around her body.

For a moment, Maya remained rigid in his hold. Then she succumbed to his warmth. To his huge protective body. She melted into him. And god, but he felt good. Like he was holding together every little part of her that threatened to break.

"Thank you," she whispered.

CHAPTER 17

*M*aya didn't feel the air that whipped her face. She'd been running for at least twenty minutes and her body had not even begun to heat.

But she didn't feel cold.

Maybe it was because a numbness had settled in her bones these last few days. It was probably her body's way of protecting itself. From the memory of the break-in, the danger that trailed her, the almost attack at the bar, and of course, the tension between her and Bodie.

The last one was entirely her fault. She was the one pushing him away still. If he had his way, she was sure they'd be sleeping in the same bed. Cuddling on the couch...

Maya shook her head. She didn't want to think about that.

They weren't together because she was a coward. She'd never known herself to be a coward before. It was a side that had snuck up on her since meeting Bodie.

Obviously, she was only a coward when feelings were involved.

It wasn't a surprise that she hadn't known about this earlier. Never in her life had she felt this way about a person. Never had she felt such fear about falling deeper. About loving a man, only to have him leave her.

She could love Bodie. He would be easy to love…unlike her.

Maya frowned at the sudden ache in her chest. She hated that it came every time she thought about him. It was the only time the numbness faded.

Maya shot a quick glance around the street, wondering where Bodie was now. He never mentioned following her, and he never left the apartment with her, but she knew he was there. Always protecting her.

She appreciated that he was fading into the background and giving her the illusion of space. The space that she so desperately needed right now.

Maya kept her pace slow, so as not to aggravate her heart. It was tough. All she wanted to do was push her body to the limit. Exhaust herself.

She had begun a new habit the last few days. Each morning, instead of just running and returning home, she would make a stop at the coffee shop. Caffeine had become a necessity. It was the one indulgence she allowed herself. If she wasn't going to let herself have Bodie, she needed coffee.

A few minutes later, Maya came to a stop in front of the shop. She took a moment to catch her breath before pushing inside.

The booth in the back corner was available. Just like it had been yesterday and the day before. It may as well have her name on it. Other people must not like being so removed from the crowd. Away from the hustle and bustle of people.

Maya did.

She was halfway there when a voice and a hand on her arm stopped her. Looking down, her gaze clashed with Shayna's.

"Hey, girl!"

"Hey, Shayna." Maya tried to hide her surprise at seeing the other woman away from the bar.

"You discovered the coffee shop! It was inevitable. This place is rad. Have a coffee with me. I need someone to tell my problems to."

Maya eyed the back booth with longing. She'd become accustomed to sitting alone. She had her own problems to ponder. It wasn't like she could say no, though. Dropping into the seat opposite Shayna, Maya pulled off her gloves.

Shayna frowned. "Your cheeks are red."

"I ran here."

Shayna appeared so shocked by that, her expression was almost comical. "You ran? In the icy winter-land of Keystone?"

"I'm addicted to running."

Shayna shook her head. "Wish *my* addiction was running."

When the other woman didn't volunteer any more information, Maya had to ask. "What's your addiction?"

"Good question." Shayna tapped her chin. "I would have to say chocolate. Especially peppermint chocolate. I'm also pretty addicted to Midori. Oh, and men. I loooove men. Especially ones with a good six-pack."

Immediately, Bodie's chiseled chest came to mind. He had a six-pack. Actually, it was probably more of an eight-pack. She didn't know if that was possible, but then, a lot was probably possible for Bodie that wasn't for normal people.

Shayna waved over the waitress, and Maya ordered a coffee.

When they were alone again, Shayna leaned across the table. "Okay, now tell me, what's going on with you and Bodie."

Ah, crap. Maya could barely think about the man without needing to rub the achy feeling in her chest. She didn't think she was up to talking about him to another person. "Nothing," she finally replied. If "nothing" entailed sex, earth-shattering confessions and running away from her feelings.

Shayna rolled her eyes. "You and that beautiful specimen have been on the rocks for days. Why?"

Was the woman psychic? "How did you—"

"It's obvious, girl. To everyone. Why aren't you with him right now?"

God, the woman would make a damn good interrogator. "Him and I just aren't going to work."

She knew straightaway Shayna wasn't going to accept that as an answer.

"That's the weakest excuse I've ever heard. The man is infatuated with you. I only need to spend a second in his company to know that. What happened?"

Maya squirmed in her seat. She didn't owe Shayna an explanation. Heck, their relationship was so new it had only just reached friendship level. But it was likely Shayna wouldn't stop until she learned what she wanted to know.

"I'm not really in a place in my life to let anyone else in right now." And she wasn't sure she ever would be.

Shayna tilted her head to the side. "Okay. I see. You're scared of commitment. Scared of getting hurt."

Yes and yes. "Aren't most people?"

"Don't know. But I certainly am." Now *that* surprised Maya. Shayna didn't seem like someone who scared easy. "I'm not scared of much, but commitment to a guy scares the crap out of me. I think it's part of my natural human drive to survive. Which, I might add, is our most powerful drive."

The waitress placed a coffee in front of Maya, but she barely noticed when Shayna continued.

"If you allow yourself to love someone, then you also give them the power to hurt you. Did you know that unrequited love destroys some people?"

That did not make Maya feel better.

Shayna lifted a shoulder as she took a sip of her coffee. "People need to make their own decisions about whether they take a risk with love, because it *is* a risk. Whether they follow their hearts or their heads when they meet someone."

Maya wasn't sure she fully trusted her faulty heart. "And you generally follow…"

"My head. Whether that's the right or wrong thing to do, who the hell knows."

Maya wrapped her chilled fingers around her coffee. She had no doubt she would regret pushing Bodie away. But her heart would be protected from future pain, at least.

"Speak of the devil."

At Shayna's words, Maya followed the other woman's gaze to the door.

There, stepping inside, was Bodie.

He'd never come in before. Even though she'd always sensed him watching, he'd remained in the shadows. Now he was heading their way. His eyes on her. Holding her captive.

~

"I'M JUST across the street from the coffee shop."

Bodie could see Maya perfectly through the shop window. She sat with Shayna while he spoke on the phone to his friend and teammate, Mason.

"She still being distant?"

"It's torture, Eagle." Torture was probably putting it lightly. "After those assholes tried to attack her outside the bar, all I wanted to do was hold her. Wrap my arms around the woman and protect her. She didn't want me."

It was killing him.

"What are you going to do?"

Other than feel sorry for himself? "Not sure. A part of me thinks I should just step back. If she doesn't want a partner, I need to accept that and just be her protector." The very thought of doing so had his insides feeling raw with pain.

"It sounds like she's had a rough time. She probably just needs some space, Red."

Bodie watched as Maya chuckled at something Shayna said. Even though he was across the street, he could see that the smile didn't quite reach her eyes. "Any news back home?"

He hoped his friend said no, because "news" usually entailed something bad. He wanted to be there to help when Hylar and his men attacked.

"Nope. No sign of Hylar or Carter's team." Carter was another former SEAL. He and his team had also been part of Project Arma. But they'd remained with Hylar after the truth came out.

"Jobs tried to get in contact with Sinclair," Mason continued. "He wanted to see if the guy has any updates—but he's on leave. Jobs spoke to the replacement, who's still getting caught up on everything."

Sinclair went on leave? "What kind of leave?"

"Jobs did some research, hacked some files. It was recorded as medical leave. Whether it actually was or not is another story."

Bodie shook his head. Sinclair was the lead CIA agent on the Project Arma case. He was, and always had been, an asshole. The guy was supposed to keep Bodie's team in the loop on what was going on with the case. He didn't. The team had researched him extensively, never finding any links between him and Project Arma.

"Go to her."

Bodie's brows pulled together at his friend's words. "What?"

"Stop watching her, walk inside that shop, and talk to her."

"She doesn't want me—"

"Or maybe she wants you to convince her that you're not going anywhere. That you care enough to stick it out."

Bodie thought he was doing just that by being present. But maybe not. "Okay, talk soon."

"You gonna do it?"

"Yes. Wish me luck."

Hanging up, he headed across the road. The moment he stepped inside, Maya's gaze clashed with his.

He stopped beside their table. "Morning, ladies. Is it okay if I join you?"

The one time he took his eyes off Maya, it was to see a megawatt smile on Shayna's face.

"Sit," she said, already pushing the spare seat out. "Before I physically shove your ass into the chair."

As soon as Bodie sat, a waitress appeared and took his coffee order. When he looked back to Maya, he noticed she was looking at her cup of coffee as if it was a newly discovered species.

"So, Bodie," Shayna said, "tell us about yourself. Any hobbies?"

Hobbies? Was chasing a deadly enemy classified as a hobby? What about protecting a woman that didn't want him near her?

"Since getting out of the military, I've really just been enjoying my freedom."

Shayna nodded. "Any women in your life?"

Wow, she didn't mess around. "There is this one woman I like." Like...was infatuated with...they were the same, weren't they?

Shayna propped her elbow on the table and her chin in her hand. "I see. And what is it exactly that you like about this woman?"

The coffee was placed in front of Bodie, and he took a sip before responding. "I like how smart she is. You don't even need to talk to her to see her intelligence. I like the gold flecks in her eyes that make them shine that much brighter. And I like her courage." From the corner of his eye, Bodie caught Maya twitch. It was subtle. So subtle, he doubted anyone else would have seen it. "She feels fear, but she doesn't let it define her."

This time, he heard her quick intake of breath. Bodie finally looked her way. She was staring right at him. With wide eyes and her mouth slightly ajar.

Shayna sighed. "That. Is so. Dang beautiful."

Bodie waited another beat before finally dragging his eyes

away from Maya. There was more he could say on the matter. But he also didn't want to push too much. She needed to decide whether a relationship with him was something she wanted to pursue on her own. And he would give her the space to do that.

CHAPTER 18

*M*aya lifted another chair onto a table.

A couple more days had passed since she'd been at the coffee shop with Bodie and Shayna. Since then, Bodie had been sweet but distant.

She should be happy. After all, it was *her* distance that had caused the strained relationship.

The fact that he'd hardly spoken to her all shift should *not* be making her feel so anxious. And the way his eyes had barely landed on her shouldn't be making her heart clench in pain.

It was better this way. There was less risk of her falling in love with the guy.

Then why was the ache in her chest starting to feel like a gaping hole?

Maya snuck a peak at Bodie from below her lashes. He was mopping the other side of the room. His eyes were downcast.

Turning away, she focused on putting up the last few chairs. He probably needed to get back to Marble Falls soon. She needed to give him an answer as to whether she would join him. The thought of him leaving town without her sent a jolt of pain through her heart.

Pausing, Maya rubbed a hand over her chest.

"Are you okay?"

At Bodie's question, her eyes shot to him. She warmed at his concern before dropping her hand. "Of course."

I'm just trying to work up the courage to move across the country with you. Drop my barriers and trust you not to break my heart.

His gaze held hers for another beat before he went back to cleaning.

The short exchange disappointed her. Never in her life had a man affected her this way.

Grabbing a cloth, Maya wiped down the bar. Bodie's back was now to her, and she had a perfect view of his perfect behind.

Did the man have to be so sexy?

Not that him being ugly would have changed how she felt about him. An unattractive exterior wouldn't take away from his kindness. Or his protective nature. Or the way he tried to make everyone around him smile.

Argh. The guy was faultless.

A small voice in her head whispered that she could keep him. That maybe this ache in her chest was love. But the sad truth was, she had no idea what love felt like.

The thought made her belly cramp.

Dropping the cloth into the sink, Maya looked around for something else to do. Something far away from the flawless man who stood too close.

Drinks. The Budweiser needed to be restocked. Grabbing them from the storage room would buy her at least a few minutes of distance. Bodie had said he would grab them later, but she needed a job to keep her mind occupied.

Maya headed down the hall and stepped into the storage room. She studied the shelves, spotting the Budweiser on a top shelf. Of course it was. It couldn't be somewhere easy like on the ground.

Grabbing the ladder, she leaned it on the shelves and began

climbing. She'd just begun shuffling the box out when she realized she'd underestimated the weight of the beer. Either that, or overestimated her own strength.

"What the hell are you doing?"

The booming voice startled her so badly; the ladder rocked against the shelves before tipping backward.

Maya closed her eyes, waiting for the pain of hitting the ground. But instead of hitting a hard floor, her body landed in warm, strong arms.

Opening her eyes, she found Bodie's face above hers as his strong arms wrapped around her back and legs. His brown eyes boring into hers. But where usually he looked at her with affection and warmth, right now, he looked annoyed. "Maya, I told you that I'd get the beer."

Being this close to Bodie, after not touching him for so many days, had tingles wandering through her abdomen. "You were busy. I needed a job."

And distance. Although, right now, the lack of distance was pure bliss.

"The cases are too heavy. Are you trying to break your neck?"

Bodie didn't wait for a response. He placed her on her feet before moving the ladder back into place and climbing up. He pulled the box out quickly and easily, making it look like it weighed nothing, especially when he shifted it to one arm and climbed down the ladder with the other.

He'd almost made it to the door when Maya found her voice. "Bodie…"

He stopped at the sound of his name and turned. The beer still firmly against his side. "What is it, Maya?"

What is it? It's that she hated that he was treating her differently. Yes, she understood that it was her fault. That he was treating her how she'd been treating him for the last week. It didn't make it any easier to accept. "You're so distant."

Bodie's eyes softened as he lowered the beer to the ground beside him. "I'm giving you space. Isn't that what you wanted?"

Yes. No. Christ, Maya didn't know what she wanted. But this didn't feel right.

"I want the old Bodie back. The one who smiles and talks to me." *The one who makes my heart gallop a million miles an hour. Who soothes my anxiety.* "I know that it's not fair of me to want that when I haven't given you either of those things, but I do."

He scrubbed a hand over his pained face. "Maya…"

Oh god, nothing good ever came from saying someone's name like that. Like they were tired of the very thought of you.

"I care about you. A lot. It's actually nuts how strong my feelings are. When I'm with you, you're all I see. So being around you, while not being able to touch you—being around you, and you not being *mine*—causes me physical pain. Like, heart-being-torn-from-chest kind of pain."

Maya's breath caught in her throat. The pain he described was exactly what she'd been feeling. When Bodie's hands lowered to his sides, Maya realized just how tired he looked. Like he'd just spent his last shred of energy.

"All I want to do is sweep you into my arms and hold you, but I'm trying to be respectful. I'm trying to accept the fact that you don't need me in the way that I need you…and it's just about destroying me."

Maya's heart pounded against her ribs, loud and hard. *This* is what she'd been running from. Words so sweet that all her walls broke down.

On the outside, she didn't move a muscle. On the inside, everything shifted. Every little part of her that had been fighting what she felt, didn't want to fight anymore.

When she continued to remain silent, Bodie's tormented expression changed to one of disappointment. Breathing out a sigh, he bent and picked up the box.

Maya took a small step forward. "I was five when I recognized that I didn't have what other people had." Bodie paused before straightening. "It was the first week of school, and the teacher asked us to draw a picture of our family. While everyone else started drawing, I sat there for a long time wondering *which* family to draw, only to stop at the knowledge that none of them were mine." Maya swallowed before continuing. "Needing another person scares me because people leave. I've survived everyone else leaving. I don't know if I could survive you. But I think I do...need you."

Actually, she knew she did. And it was terrifying.

Suddenly, Maya felt exposed and vulnerable.

Bodie moved to her. So close, she could feel his warm breath on her face. "You're not someone I feel capable of walking away from. Not now. Not ever."

He said the words firmly, making her believe him. Despite everything life had exposed her to.

Bodie reached out a hand and placed it on the back of her neck.

Oh, how she'd missed the feel of his skin on hers. It had only been days, but it felt like so much longer. Reaching up, Maya slid her fingers through his hair. "It might take my damaged heart a bit longer than most."

Bodie lowered his head so that his lips hovered above hers. "You can have all the time in the world."

The moment their lips touched, Maya hummed. The kiss soothed the ache in her chest. It quieted the ugly voices in her head.

The kiss was healing.

His hand skimmed her waist before lowering to her butt and lifting her up against him.

Almost instinctively, Maya wrapped her legs around his waist, causing her skirt to bunch at her hips. Then there was a wall pressed to her back and Bodie pressed to her front.

His lips never left hers. This kiss felt different from the

others. Hungrier. Like they both wanted to recapture every lost second from the last several days.

Maya ground her body against his, a fiery need growing inside her.

When Bodie's hand lifted her shirt, grabbing her breast, she whimpered against his mouth. Then he began to squeeze, massaging her. Lower, at her core, even though there was a barrier of clothing, she could feel every ridge of his body.

His kiss deepened, his tongue exploring her mouth. His breathing hard. Bodie yanked her bra cup down. Then his mouth tore from hers and was on her nipple. Sucking and tugging.

Yes. Yes to Bodie, and to this, and to them together.

When the sharp edge of his teeth grazed her sensitive peak, she threw her head back and released a soft cry. She ran her fingers through his hair, grinding her core against him. The apex between her thighs ached. Every movement only heightened her need.

"I need you, Bodie."

His mouth trailed back up until it reached her neck. At the same time, his hand reached down. At the firm pressure of his thumb against her clit, Maya's whole body vibrated against his and her stomach quivered.

While his mouth continued to suck her neck, his fingers played with her. Her body started to scream with need.

Then his finger was pushing inside her. Filling her.

She clawed at his shoulders, blood roaring through her veins. His thumb moved against her clit while he pushed in and out. He continued like that for several minutes, pushing her close to the edge. Driving her crazy.

Bodie slid in a second finger.

God. Her body was so heated with need, she was close to exploding.

"Bodie…"

When he didn't stop, didn't so much as pause, Maya tugged

his head up and kissed him again. She ground herself on his hand while thoroughly tasting him.

"I want you," she whispered, her breath brushing his lips. "Inside me."

He growled. Removing his hand from her body, he quickly opened his pants, shoving them down, then pushed her underwear to the side before sliding inside her.

Pleasure shot through her body as her muscles stretched to accommodate him.

Then he was moving. Pulling out until just the tip touched her before pushing back inside.

Arching her back, Maya surrendered herself to the sensations. To the intensity.

His thrusts remained steady. She tightened her legs around him, pulling his body closer, urging him to go faster.

When he finally did, Maya cried out at the electricity coursing through her core.

Maya was consumed by the insatiable need within her. By the man who made her want so much more than she ever thought she'd have.

Bodie lifted a hand to cup her breast and pinched her nipple with his thumb and finger.

Maya exploded. Her whole body convulsed and spasmed around him as she called out his name in passion. Her blood roared in her ears as her muscles strained. Her breathing heavy as Bodie tensed inside her.

He quickly pulled out and growled deep in his throat as he climaxed.

It took a while for both their bodies to steady. For the throbbing to dull and their breathing to ease. Once they did, they still didn't part. He still held her tightly.

Maya surrendered to the fact that she was Bodie's, and he was hers.

CHAPTER 19

*B*odie left the bedroom with a smile on his face. Maya was his. She hadn't said those exact words, but she may as well have. Everything that had happened last night confirmed it.

It had taken them a while to get back to packing up the bar, but once it was all done, they'd returned to Bodie's place, where she'd slept in his arms. It had been the first decent chunk of sleep he'd gotten in almost a week.

God, he could get used to mornings like this. Waking up with her beside him. Listening to her heart beating...incredible. And better yet, today was Monday, and they both had the day off.

There was a fair at Keystone Lake this week. Maya had said she wanted to go ice skating, so this would be the perfect opportunity.

Not that Bodie was any good at ice skating. He'd probably fall on his ass a dozen times, but if it made Maya smile, he didn't care.

Moving into the kitchen, he started on breakfast while Maya got ready.

He needed to broach the topic of her moving to Marble Falls

again. Every day that passed with him not being there made him nervous. His team was strongest together.

Just before he'd left, the team had blocked Hylar from getting his hands on some drugs. Drugs he needed to create more DNA-altered soldiers. The team expected backlash. So far, there hadn't been a peep from the guy. That wasn't to say nothing was coming, though.

That was the main reason Bodie was so keen to get back to his team. But also, because Maya being in Marble Falls would be an extra layer of protection. An extra seven layers.

Bodie couldn't help but be excited to introduce Maya to his team. He'd meant what he said last night. He couldn't see himself leaving Maya. Ever. The guys would understand; they knew how much he wanted what they had.

He paused while cutting bread when shuffling noises sounded from the hall. The shuffling was accompanied by three heart-beats. The sounds stopped right outside his apartment door.

He tensed, adrenaline rushing through his body. He wasn't expecting company.

Bodie opened a drawer and dug under the tea towels for his gun. Moving silently to the door, he took a quiet breath, then looked through the peephole.

The tension immediately released from his body, and he quickly tugged the door open.

In front of him stood three familiar faces. All smiling.

Actually, no, Wyatt and Oliver were smiling. Quinn was looking at the gun in surprise.

Bodie frowned. "What the hell?"

Quinn's jaw dropped. *"You're* saying what the hell to *us*? You just waltz out here with a gun in hand." She looked up at Wyatt. "And you're smiling?"

Wyatt dropped an arm around Quinn's shoulders, pressing a kiss to her head. The smile on his face remained. "He's got reflexes as good as me, Quinn. He wouldn't have shot you."

She didn't look so convinced, but Wyatt's words seemed to soothe her somewhat.

Shaking his head, Bodie returned to the kitchen, stashing the gun while everyone came inside. "What are you guys doing here?" Not that Bodie was complaining. Seeing his friends was like bringing a part of home to Keystone. His anxious ass could have used a little warning though.

Oliver dropped onto the couch. "We're here to drag you home. You and Maya. We need to be together."

Exactly what Bodie had just been thinking.

"And to see if you need help," Wyatt added.

Bodie lifted a brow. "Please don't take this the wrong way, but I'm not sure Quinn will be much help against Hylar."

Quinn opened her mouth, clearly about to give him a piece of her mind, when Wyatt jumped in. "Quinn felt up to traveling and—"

"My brother finally let me out of his sight," she finished, rolling her eyes. "I would have been here earlier had Mr. Protective not been around."

Oliver scoffed from his place on the couch. "She basically refused to stay home any longer."

Quinn nodded, clearly satisfied with that answer.

Bodie ran a hand through his hair. "You couldn't have called?" It would have saved him from almost pulling a gun on his friends.

"We could have," Oliver said, now lounging back on the couch with his feet on the coffee table. "We decided it was more fun this way."

"It was a last-minute decision," Wyatt added. "We spoke to Eagle and he agreed you needed help."

That was not the message Bodie had been trying to convey during their last phone conversation.

From the other room, he heard the shower turn off.

"She should be out in a sec," Bodie said, more for Quinn's

benefit because she couldn't hear what they could. "She's been through a lot, so go gently with her."

Maya wasn't made of glass, Bodie knew that, but with all she'd been through and her heart health, he wanted to make things as smooth as possible for her from this point on.

～

MAYA RUBBED a hand over her chest as she glanced at her reflection in the bathroom mirror. Even though she'd woken ridiculously happy about her relationship with Bodie, she'd also woken feeling short of breath. She wanted to curse out the hole in her heart. Usually, after a solid night's sleep, she felt okay.

She'd been so close. If the damn lab break-in hadn't happened, she would have already had the surgery she needed. Unfortunately, the procedure had been scheduled for one week after the break-in.

She'd had no choice but to miss it. If she hadn't run, if she hadn't disappeared, she doubted she would have lived long enough for the surgery anyway.

Now, every day that passed was another that extra blood was being pumped to her lungs. The extra blood meant that her heart and lungs needed to work harder, which in turn increased her risk for a whole lot of not-so-great stuff. Things like stroke and heart failure and pulmonary hypertension were just a few of them.

Maya had saved herself from being caught and killed, but by running, she'd lost her job with the pharmaceutical company, and with it her health insurance. That meant she no longer had the means to pay for the procedure.

So, in saving her life, she'd effectively also thrown it into question.

Maya hadn't told Bodie about the extent of her heart problem. Today. She needed to do so today.

She also needed to tell him something else. About the faceless man she was running from. At first, she'd hidden that small detail to protect him. Then, since telling her about his abilities, her mind had been filled with...everything.

Now that she'd decided to trust him again, Maya wanted there to be no secrets between them. The sooner she told him, the better.

Moving back into the bedroom, Maya had just pulled a sweater over her shirt when she heard voices from the living room. Unfamiliar male voices. Frowning, she drew closer to the door.

When a woman's voice sounded, she paused. It was a voice she remembered.

Quinn. The reporter for *The New York Times*.

Opening the bedroom door, Maya stepped into the room. Bodie stood in the living room with Quinn, who had a man close beside her. Another man sat on the couch. Both guys were all muscles. Just like Bodie.

Everyone in the room went quiet and looked at Maya. The sudden attention almost made her nervous. Then she glanced at Bodie. Saw the smile stretching his lips before he moved to her side and placed an arm around her waist. She instantly calmed.

"Maya, these are some of my friends from Marble Falls. This is Wyatt." Bodie pointed to the man who was standing. "We call him Jobs, because he's a whiz with IT. This is Oliver—Ax, to the guys." Maya glanced at the green-eyed man who was studying her from the couch. "And you've met Quinn."

Maya shifted her gaze to Quinn. The woman looked exactly the same as when she'd met her in the diner months ago. The only difference was that maybe she looked a bit more relaxed. Happier.

Before Maya could say a word, Quinn walked forward and wrapped her arms around her. The hug wasn't tentative or shy. It was firm and warm and friendly. Like Quinn was greeting an old friend she hadn't seen in a while.

It took Maya a moment to snap out of her surprise and return the hug.

"I am so glad that you're okay," Quinn said softly. "I was so worried."

"You were worried about me?" She still wasn't completely used to people being worried about her.

"Of course! I told you I'd help you. No, I swore that I would. So when I went to the address you gave me but you weren't there…" She put her hand to her chest. "You have no idea the fear and guilt I've been going through."

"You barely know me."

"Not true. We emailed back and forth for a while. I felt like I got to know you at least a little bit. Plus, you came to meet me even though it put you in danger. You trusted me to save more people." Quinn sighed. "I'm just so glad Bodie found you. That you're safe."

Warmth filtered through Maya's chest. If it hadn't been for Quinn, Bodie never would have known she existed. So Maya felt like she should be thanking the other woman.

"Thank you, Quinn. For helping someone you barely knew."

She smiled. "I intend to get to know you a lot better. You and I are going to be great friends."

Oliver chuckled from the couch. "Whether you want to be or not."

Quinn leaned closer. "Ignore him. I usually do."

Maya couldn't help but laugh. Unfortunately, the laugh was followed by a cough from her tight chest.

Bodie put his hand to her shoulder. "You okay?"

She forced a smile. "I'm okay." By the look on Bodie's face, he didn't believe her one bit. "Should we make breakfast for everyone?"

Distraction seemed the best idea. Maya had things she needed to tell Bodie, but now, when his friends had just arrived, was not the time.

Thankfully, everyone headed to the kitchen. Bodie's concerned look lasted another beat before he slid his arm around her waist and tugged her in the same direction.

CHAPTER 20

*B*odie stepped off the ice with Wyatt at his side. They'd only been on the ice for ten minutes, but he already wanted a break. Watching the women skate felt a whole lot more fun to him than falling on his ass.

Sitting down, Bodie and Wyatt replaced their skates for shoes, all the while keeping the women in their vision. Oliver had skipped the ice-skating to do a perimeter check.

It was midafternoon. They'd been at the fair for a couple of hours but had spent most of that time eating burritos and sitting for a caricaturist. This was the first physically exerting activity Maya had attempted, and he didn't think she'd last long.

Once they both had shoes on, Bodie and Wyatt leaned against the railing and watched Maya and Quinn glide on the ice. Both women had smiles on their faces.

"Do you hear it?" Bodie asked, without drawing his gaze from Maya.

"The whooshing in her chest?" It didn't surprise Bodie that his friend didn't need to ask to know what he was referring to. "I did."

Bodie had heard it at other times. Today it was louder. More constant.

Wyatt ran a hand through his hair. "Did you ask her about it?"

Yes. That was the annoying part. "The couple of times we've been alone today, I tried asking if she was okay. Even specifically mentioned her heart. Both times she said we'd talk later."

He knew that today was about fun, but her safety was his priority. If she had something she needed to talk to him about, if something was wrong, he wanted to know *now*.

"The woman clearly likes to keep her cards close to her chest. It's no surprise she doesn't want to say anything around people she's just met. We'll get a room at a hotel tonight. Give you guys some privacy."

The offer brought Bodie some relief. His friends had planned to take the spare room and the couch, but Bodie and Maya needed time to talk about her health. He scrubbed a hand over his face. "Her breathing's been off today, too."

"I can do a deeper check on her medical history if you want?"

Did Bodie want that? It was tempting. But it was also an over-step. He wanted Maya to talk to him. If a relationship with the woman was the goal, trust between them was important.

"I'll see how tonight goes." Wyatt would be his last resort.

His friend nodded.

Bodie shot a quick glance around. "Ax must be sick of us to have disappeared for so long."

"Maybe he got distracted by a woman during his check."

A smile tugged at Bodie's lips. It wasn't a surprise that Oliver and Kye were the last single men standing. Neither of them had ever shown the slightest interest in pursuing anything long-term with a woman.

Wyatt clamped a hand on Bodie's shoulder. "I'm glad you've found someone who makes you happy, my friend. You deserve it."

The smile on Bodie's face grew. "We're new, and we have stuff to work through. Her health being one of them. Her moving to

Marble Falls another. But I care about her." Bodie paused. "I think I might be falling in love with her."

Every moment he spent with her just confirmed it.

"Nothing crazy about that. Love doesn't know time and it doesn't ask permission. It just hits you square in the face."

That was damn true. "It's different to how I thought it would be."

"How so?"

"I thought love would touch one part of me. Maybe the part of my heart that had been vacant." How wrong he'd been. "I feel it everywhere. This all-consuming need to be with her. To protect and love her. It's wrecked me. But at the same time, it's breathed new life into me."

Wyatt's lips stretched into a smile. "That's love."

"Lucky that Rocket was the first to experience it. If I hadn't seen you guys go through it, I might have been scared of its intensity."

"Rocket's fearless."

Yes, he was. "Have him and Evie set a date for the big day yet?"

Luca, Rocket to the team, was the first in the group to meet the love of his life. They'd gotten engaged not that long ago. Everyone on the team was eager to know when the couple was tying the knot.

"Nope. He's thinking of having a ceremony with just us and a bigger wedding later. I think the guy's on edge that it will never happen. He's sick of waiting."

Bodie scowled. "If we could just find that asshole Hylar, we wouldn't need to put our lives on hold or hesitate over big decisions."

It wasn't enough that their former commander had to impact their pasts by injecting them with experimental drugs, he also had to affect their present.

"I feel your rage, brother. He'll get what's coming to him."

That needed to be true. For everyone's sake.

Taking his eyes from Maya, Bodie scanned the area. He was about to turn his attention back to the rink when something caught his eye…or someone. Someone familiar.

The person disappeared before Bodie could be sure it was him.

Straightening, Bodie studied the crowd, searching. After a few seconds, he caught sight of the man again.

"We have company."

He felt the shift in Wyatt straightaway. From relaxed to alert. "Who?"

"Agent Sinclair."

Wyatt swore under his breath. "What the hell is he doing here? He's supposed to be on leave."

"The asshole's watching us," Bodie said with deadly calm.

"Or watching Maya?" Wyatt suggested.

Sinclair had been searching for Maya since the lab break-in. She was the only surviving witness, but she'd disappeared, leaving the agent short of answers.

Bodie took a step toward the crowd. "You watch the women. I'll go."

He'd find out why the agent was here. And if it was for Maya, Sinclair would need to get on board with the fact that Bodie wasn't leaving her side. Not for a second.

"Guess they couldn't hack the ice any longer."

Maya laughed at Quinn's comment. "I don't ever want to leave. Don't get me wrong, I'm very aware of how terrible I am. You and Bodie have had to scrape me off the ice more times than I care to count. But I love it. Choosing Keystone was a good decision."

She'd researched towns extensively. The moment the image of

a frozen Keystone Lake had popped up, her decision had been made.

"You like skating?" Quinn asked.

"This is my first time…don't tell me you didn't notice."

Quinn's brow furrowed in surprise. "Well, you're a quick learner."

Yeah, right. Maya wasn't even going to pretend to believe the other woman. "It's okay, I know I suck. It doesn't bother me."

Quinn laughed.

Maya shrugged. "I always wanted to go ice skating but I've never had the opportunity." Growing up, no foster family had taken her skating. Then she'd spent her adult life studying and working. "I wanted my own Lorelai moment."

"Your own Lorelai moment?"

Maya chuckled. "I watched a lot of *Gilmore Girls* growing up, and Lorelai had this love for snow. There's this one scene where Luke builds her a skating rink in her own backyard. When she skated on it, she was just so…happy."

And free.

"Your parents never took you?"

"I grew up in foster care." Maya slowed as they approached the turn. This is where she usually hit the ice with her butt. "None of the families ever took me."

Quinn reached out and clasped Maya's hand. Over the day, she'd slowly started to get used to the other woman's easy affection. "Now you have Bodie and us."

Her heart warmed at Quinn's words. The other woman was easy to like.

As Maya breathed in her next breath, she felt the familiar constriction of her airways. Even though they'd taken it relatively easy over the day, the tightness hadn't faded.

She rubbed a hand over her chest.

Quinn's hand tightened around hers. "You okay?"

Just like she had with Bodie, Maya smiled and nodded. She

needed to tell Bodie what she was feeling. That's exactly what she intended to do once they were alone tonight. "I'm okay."

Quinn's intelligent eyes studied Maya's face. "Are you sure? Because I remember you telling me you had a heart defect. I looked it up, it can be pretty serious depending on how large the hole is."

"You looked it up?"

"Of course. I was worried about you."

It still astounded Maya that she and Quinn had only met once, but she'd clearly left an impact on the other woman. "That's nice of you to be worried. It's probably just a bit too much exercise for my unfit butt, but do you mind if we have a break?"

"Of course," Quinn said, as they headed to the exit. "And Bodie told Wyatt about your morning runs. Trust me, if either of us gets the label of 'unfit,' it's me."

When they reached the edge of the rink, Maya spotted Bodie moving away from Wyatt and into the crowd. Quinn walked straight into Wyatt's waiting arms. Even with her skates on, she wasn't close to reaching his height.

Maya sat on the bench. "Where did Bodie get to?"

When Wyatt was silent for a few moments, she looked up to see him studying the crowd.

Quinn sat beside her. "He's probably trying to isolate the sounds. Listening to something."

"Got you." Wyatt said the words under his breath, but both Maya and Quinn heard.

Once Maya's shoes were on, she searched for Bodie in the crowd. It only took her a few seconds to spot him. He came in and out of view as people milled around him.

He wasn't alone. He was talking to a man who stood a couple of inches shorter than him. They were across the park and a fair distance away.

Standing, she placed her hands on her hips. Wyatt remained

silent. If he could hear the conversation from that far, and with all the people, Maya would be seriously impressed.

Maya turned to Quinn, who stood as well. "Do you know who that guy is?"

Quinn shook her head. "No clue. By the expression on Mr. Serious' face here, it's someone important."

Wyatt pulled his phone from his pocket. "I'm just gonna call Ax." He took a step away from both Maya and Quinn.

Just then, the tightening in Maya's chest worsened to the point her breath was stolen completely. Leaning over, she placed her hands on her knees.

God, it rarely got this bad.

Quinn put a hand on her back. "Hey! You okay?"

No. She didn't think she was. Her body needed rest. "Do you think Bodie will mind if I interrupt him? I don't feel very good?"

Quinn turned her head, making a gesture to Wyatt that they were going to Bodie before turning back to Maya. "Let's get a bit closer and see if we can get his attention."

Nodding, Maya straightened. As they drew closer, she studied the other man's face. There was nothing remarkable about him. He was of average height, with brown hair and eyes. Fit, but nowhere near Bodie's level of fit. But he had a look about him. A look that made Maya almost certain he was accustomed to being listened to.

Definitely a man of authority.

They were halfway there when the sound of his voice drifted in their direction. It was faint over the noise of the crowd—but it had her feet freezing to the spot.

She'd heard that voice before. Not only in real life, but also in her nightmares. It had been on repeat for months. Tormenting her day and night.

Ringing sounded in her ears. So loud that every other noise was wiped out.

Quinn moved directly in front of her, grabbing Maya's arms.

But she barely saw or felt the other woman. Every muscle in her body screamed at her to run. To get away from the danger. She took a hurried step back. Then another. Her breaths were coming out in short pants.

Go!

Her brain screamed the word before she began moving. Away from *him*.

Agent Sinclair.

Maya weaved her way through the crowd. Dammit, people kept getting in her way! Bumping into her. Slowing her down.

Why was Bodie speaking to him? Did they know each other? Had they worked together? Oh god! She hoped not.

Slow. She felt way too slow. She forced her feet to move faster. She was vaguely aware of the pain in her chest increasing. That she was barely getting air to her lungs. But that was secondary. Getting away was the priority.

Maya was now running. She darted through the flock of people like she was being chased by an army. The fear cascading through her mind was blinding.

She'd made it to the outskirts of the fair when she collided with a large body.

Oliver held her arms tightly, stopping her from rebounding back onto the ground. When Maya tried to pull away, his fingers tightened like manacles. "Whoa, darlin'. Everything okay?"

No. Everything was far from okay.

She opened her mouth to tell him exactly that but she couldn't, because all her energy was being spent on her breaths.

"Breathe. In and out."

She tried. Oh lord, did she try. "I-I can't."

Oliver wrapped his arms around her. One moment they were out in the open, the next they were standing in a quiet corner in between two buildings.

She felt the coolness of a wall behind her and the warmth of his hand on her arm. With his other hand, he pulled out his phone and pressed some keys before shoving it back in his pocket.

Darkness was starting to dim her vision.

She was going to pass out.

"No...no hospital." She gasped the words to him. If she passed out, and he took her to a hospital, the agent would find her more easily. But what if they were all friends with him? He'd find her anyway.

She could see Oliver's mouth moving, but the buzzing in her ears had grown louder.

She turned her head just in time to see Bodie running toward them. Before he could reach her, she lost consciousness.

CHAPTER 21

*B*odie hung up the phone. He'd just spent the last twenty minutes talking to Sage, who was both their team doctor and Mason's woman.

Oliver moved to stand beside Bodie. "Her heart rate's gone down. Her breathing is back to normal. Now we'll monitor her, and if she's not awake within a couple of hours, we'll take her to the hospital."

Wyatt nodded from across the room. "Saving her immediate life takes priority over her request of no hospital."

Their words made sense. But it didn't change the fact that watching her lie unconscious in his bed made him long to do more.

When Bodie had looked away from Sinclair at the fair, only to see Wyatt on the phone but no sign of the women, dread had overridden everything else and he'd taken off looking for her, leaving Sinclair right where he was. The moment he saw Maya fall unconscious into Oliver's arms, a fear he'd never felt before had cascaded through his entire body.

They'd taken her straight to his apartment. Bodie had wanted the hospital but her final words had stopped him. Had her heart rate stayed as high as it had been, Bodie would have ignored her request and taken her anyway. As it was, once they'd reached the car, once he'd held her in his arms, her breaths had evened out and some color returned to her cheeks.

Sitting on the edge of the bed, he touched Maya's hand. Warmth had also returned to her skin, thank god.

He shot a look across the room. "Can you take me through the lead up to this again, Quinn?" So he could try to make sense of how one minute, Maya was fine, and the next she was the furthest from it.

Quinn had talked about it in the car but he'd barely heard. His entire focus had been on the air moving in and out of Maya's chest. The sound of her heart beating.

She cleared her throat from her position under Wyatt's arm. "When we were on the ice, she started rubbing her chest like she was in pain. She looked worried. We decided to rest, so we got off the ice. When Wyatt went to call Oliver, I think her chest pains got worse because she wanted to go home."

Guilt swirled in Bodie's chest. He'd talked to Sinclair for too long. He should have kept an eye on Maya, dammit. He knew something had been wrong.

"We were about halfway to you when she just stopped walking. Her face went white—like, *white*-white. I tried asking her what was wrong but it was like she couldn't hear me. Then she turned around and started walking through the crowd. I tried following, but when she started running…"

Wyatt leaned down and pressed a kiss to Quinn's head. "You did good, sunshine."

Why did Maya run? Most people who were experiencing chest pain would have stopped and rested.

Quinn shook her head. "She looked scared."

"She looked *terrified* when I caught her," Oliver added.

Bodie turned and shared a look with Oliver. His friend was likely thinking the same thing he was. "Sinclair," he muttered.

Oliver nodded. "That's what I'm thinking. He would have been involved in the investigation of the lab break-in in New York. Maybe Maya remembered him and thought he'd drag her back there."

But would that really warrant so much fear?

"We'll ask her when she wakes," Wyatt said, almost seeming to read Bodie's thoughts.

He nodded, scrubbing a hand to his face. He hoped that was soon. Not just because he wanted to get to the bottom of what happened, but also because her not waking was causing unease to pulse through his limbs.

"I might go order us some food," Quinn said softly, heading toward the door.

Wyatt took a step to follow. "You gonna stay here, Red?"

There was absolutely nowhere else he wanted to be. "I'm going to stay with her until she wakes." And even then, he probably wouldn't be leaving her side for a long time. "You and Quinn grab the spare room and Oliver take the couch. I'd prefer that you guys stay here, if that's okay."

Oliver clamped a hand to Bodie's shoulder. "Wasn't planning on going anywhere else. Give us a shout if you need anything."

Once the bedroom door was closed and it was just him and Maya, Bodie quickly removed his shirt and jeans and climbed into bed beside her. Then he pulled Maya's body against his and breathed her in. He wouldn't sleep. He'd listen to every little breath she took. He'd keep her warm.

He placed his lips near her ear. "Come back to me, sweetheart."

Because I need you to tell me that you're okay.

"It's time to take her to the hospital."

Bodie's voice sounded like it was coming to her through a tunnel. Hollow and echoey.

Her tired body almost wanted to ignore it and keep sleeping. Almost. It was the word "hospital" that pulled at her mind, forcing her attention. She didn't want a hospital. Not only could she not afford a hospital, but there were no circumstances in which she wanted them to run her name through the system.

She was sure Sinclair would have set up alerts for something like that. He would have her location within minutes.

But wait. He'd already found her...

Fragments of her last memory started coming back to her. Of the fair. Of seeing *him*. She'd heard his voice. His real voice, not the one in her head. She'd also finally seen his face.

Her heart sped up at the memory.

"I think she's waking."

That wasn't Bodie's voice, but it was familiar.

When something touched her cheek—a hand, maybe—Maya flinched.

"Maya, it's me. Bodie. Can you open those beautiful eyes for me?"

Bodie's smooth, calm voice immediately went a long way toward soothing her. But opening her eyes meant facing reality. A reality where Sinclair was right here in Keystone and had been talking to the man she was falling for.

At that thought, her eyes flew open. Bodie's face hovered above her. He was sitting on the edge of the bed. Worry lines marred his normally smooth features.

"There you are." His thumb moved over her cheek bone, lightly grazing the skin. "How are you feeling?"

Sick. Anxious. Like her world was caving in on itself.

"How do you know Sinclair?" The words fell from her lips, each one coated with fear.

Bodie's thumb paused in its movement as he studied her face. "Sinclair is the agent we're working with to locate the last remaining members of Project Arma. Was he the person who questioned you after the New York break-in?"

No. He hadn't wanted to question her. He'd wanted something else.

At her lengthy silence, someone across the room coughed. Oliver. He stood by the door.

"I'm gonna head out. Let you guys talk."

Bodie nodded, while Maya remained silent. It wasn't until it was just her and Bodie that she pushed to sit up.

"Maya—"

"I'm okay. I want to be sitting for this conversation."

She had no idea why. Maybe because being eye level would stop her from feeling at such a disadvantage. That was the last thing she wanted, when these next words were so important.

"There was something I left out when I told Quinn my story." Something that had been the driving force in her picking up and leaving New York. "Since you told me the truth about who you are and what you're doing here, I've had a lot to work through. That's the only reason I haven't told you yet. And before that...I wouldn't have mentioned it because I know how powerful the CIA is."

And she didn't want him to get hurt. The same reason she didn't tell Quinn.

Bodie became unnaturally still. When she hesitated again, he seemed to snap out of it and took her hand in his. It gave her the last bit of strength she needed.

"When the men broke into the lab, they asked for certain materials. The ones I told Quinn about. Then they called someone." A shiver coursed down Maya's spine at the memory. "While two of the guys filled a bag, the one on the phone confirmed they had what they needed. The man on the other end told them to kill us and get out."

Maya almost wished the guy hadn't put the call on speaker.

He'd probably done it so his friends could hear...or maybe because he enjoyed the fear coming off her and her coworkers.

Maya still remembered the absolute terror that had rocked her body at hearing those words. At hearing someone sign her death warrant.

Bodie remained silent, waiting for her to continue.

"They threw me against a wall and I became unconscious. When I woke up, I was in the hospital. There were people outside my door. I heard *his* voice." Her stomach clenched at the memory. "He was talking to the doctor, who told him I would wake in a few hours and to give me that time before any questioning—the doctor called him Agent Sinclair."

There was the smallest tightening of Bodie's fingers around hers and a slight narrowing of his eyes. "What happened next?"

"I assume the doctor walked away, because Sinclair's voice changed. Lowered, like he was talking to someone in confidence. I could barely hear him." But she had been able to make out a couple of words. "I heard 'atrial septal defect' and a mention of that evening."

It was enough to know she had to leave. Hell, just the sound of his voice had been enough.

"When their voices started getting farther away, I got out of bed, changed and climbed out the window. I didn't go back to my apartment, I just took out as much cash as I could from an ATM and left. I checked my emails from a public computer one last time, and that's when I saw Quinn's email. I wrote it down before leaving town."

Bodie nodded. She could tell he was trying to contain his anger. "It was smart not to go back to your apartment. Smart to run away. You did really good, sweetheart."

Maya swallowed. There was a question that she was pretty sure she knew the answer to but needed to ask anyway. "What's your relationship with Sinclair?"

Finally, all attempts to mask his emotions vanished. A scowl of rage and frustration crossed his face. The man looked ready to kill. "We've suspected for a while that he's up to something. He's never liked our involvement in shutting down Project Arma and frequently withheld information he was supposed to share. He's also just an overall asshole. We did searches on the guy but always came up with no red flags." Bodie shook his head. "When I spoke to him at the fair, he said he was in town looking for you. He had more questions about the break-in."

Sinclair would know it was a plausible reason for him being here.

"I asked how he'd found you, but when I looked over and didn't see you or Quinn, I took off before he could answer." He pressed a kiss to her temple. "Leave Sinclair to my team. You focus on you. You're safe now, Maya. He won't touch you."

His words were exactly what she needed to hear. What she'd been yearning to hear for so long. Moisture filled her eyes. "I've been so scared. Scared of the lengths he would go, to make sure I didn't talk. The power he has as both a CIA agent and with his connection to people so physically capable...I was also scared that by telling you, I'd endanger your life."

Bodie lifted his hand to her cheek. "You don't need to be scared anymore. And always tell me. Even if you think it's dangerous. Even if you're terrified for your life or mine. Tell me."

A tear spilled down her cheek. "Okay. Thank you."

Bodie pulled her to his chest.

The tough discussions weren't over. Soon, he would want to know about the severity of her heart defect. And she wanted to tell him. But for now, being held by the only man in the world who made her feel safe was too good to pull away from.

CHAPTER 22

*B*odie watched the trees pass through the window. They were a blur. Oliver wasn't speeding per se, but he definitely wasn't driving slowly.

Most people would barely be able to see a thing in the pitch-black night. Bodie could see everything, right down to the browning leaves that lay scattered at the foot of the trees.

After all, what kind of a genetically enhanced soldier wouldn't have night-vision?

"We're almost there," Oliver said, taking another right turn.

Just like Bodie, his friends had been solemn since finding out the truth about Sinclair.

Wyatt had gotten straight on the phone to Evie. The two of them had already researched the guy extensively. They knew they weren't going to find anything new in his background. This time, they focused on his movements over the last month. They wanted to know where he'd been and, more importantly, where he was right now.

Bodie shook his head. "We knew the guy was dirty. We should have done more to confirm it. Tailed him. Set up surveillance on his home. Something."

At the very least, they would have discovered that two weeks ago, it hadn't just been Sinclair who'd taken a leave of absence—six of his men were also on leave.

It was important that Bodie and Oliver didn't take long tonight. He didn't want to be away from Maya for a second longer than necessary. Not when they didn't know where those six other men were.

"His place would be swept for surveillance regularly. The CIA would make sure of it."

It was true. They should probably count themselves lucky that Maya had found out about Sinclair and exposed him.

They hadn't told anyone from the CIA what they knew. Not yet. They didn't know how deep the corruption went.

"All those years ago, when Project Arma was raided, when Hylar and his team managed to escape before police arrived, it must have been Sinclair who gave everyone the heads-up." Bodie only just held on to the curse that threatened to leave his lips.

Oliver nodded. "We finally know where the leak was."

It was that warning that had allowed Project Arma to remain active. It was because of Sinclair that Bodie's team had been hunting their enemy for so long.

His voice hardened. "I hope he's here."

He caught the slight tightening of Oliver's fingers on the wheel. "Me too, Red. But something tells me that would be too easy."

True. And when had anything been easy for them?

Wyatt and Evie had spent the entire evening researching Sinclair's movement. They'd hacked every business surveillance camera in the area and employed facial recognition software. They'd also searched for accommodations and any local buildings that might be empty.

That's how Evie had discovered the place where they were heading now. A house located in a forested section of Keystone.

The owner had passed away a year ago and since then, it had been uninhabited. Or at least, was *supposed* to be uninhabited.

It could still be empty. But about a week ago, the power was reconnected, despite the house not being sold or rented. That right there was a red flag.

The house would be a smart choice. It was close enough to make it into town quickly, but far enough away so that neighbors wouldn't realize strange men had moved in.

"Do you think his men are like us?" Oliver asked.

Bodie knew what Oliver was asking. Had his men received the same DNA-altering drugs? Probably. "I think we should expect the worst."

And hopefully be pleasantly surprised if the worst didn't come to pass.

"Are you worried about Maya?"

Always. "Yes. I'd be lying if I said I wasn't. I'm worried about her health and also her safety. I know how strong we are, but every time we think we have our women protected, Hylar or his men get around us."

There was a short pause before Oliver spoke. "He's been testing us, there's no doubt about it. But we've survived everything that's been thrown our way. And every time someone's life has been threatened, we've gotten them back. Safely."

It was true. Yet it did nothing to ease Bodie's anxiety. "Lucky you don't have someone to worry about. It will age you ten years."

At least.

When Oliver remained silent for too long, Bodie turned to study his friend. "Am I wrong?"

Oliver chuckled softly. "I don't have anyone. I'm a lone wolf, remember?" Then, after more silence, "There was this one woman, though…I met her a few weeks ago. We only spent the weekend together, heck it was actually only one night, but damn, did she leave an impression."

Bodie tried to hide his surprise. "You keep in contact?"

"Nah. We exchanged numbers. She never called, and when I tried her number, it was disconnected."

"Damn. I'm sorry, brother."

Oliver ran a hand through his hair. "Nothing to be sorry about. I'm still happy being single. I left her a note in her pocket when we parted, telling her to contact me at Marble Protection if she couldn't get through to me on my cell. What I'm feeling is probably just a bruised ego."

"I guess that can happen when you give a woman two ways to contact you and she gives you a fake number."

Oliver chuckled again. "Kind of screams 'not interested' doesn't it?"

He pulled off the highway and onto a long stretch of what once was a dirt road. It was now covered in a thick layer of snow. Oliver didn't drive far. Instead, he pulled the car to the side of the road behind the cover of trees.

It was safer to walk the remaining distance. If someone like them was at the house, they might hear Bodie and Oliver coming, regardless. They were still hoping that Sinclair and his men were fully human, but weren't holding their breaths.

They stepped out of the car and made their way through the forest. Bodie was damn glad he had a high cold threshold because a normal person would be freezing right now without the proper snow gear, which wasn't an option. It would restrict his movement if he needed to fight.

They moved quickly and quietly. For most people, the walk would be hard and slow. For them, it was the opposite.

When a break in the trees appeared, they immediately spotted the house. It was obvious the place had been uninhabited for a while. Hell, he wouldn't be surprised if it hadn't been properly kept *before* the owner died. Rotting wood covered the exterior walls and plants had begun growing between the roof shingles.

One side of the building seemed to be sinking and cracks were visible in the windows.

Bodie paused. He listened for footsteps. Heartbeats. Breaths. Anything that would indicate a person was inside.

There was silence. All he heard were Oliver's and his own heartbeats.

They moved toward the house. Bodie reached the door first and tried the handle. Unlocked.

Stepping inside, he scanned the interior. It was old and basic. A couch sat in front of him and a wooden table to the right. Beyond the table was an old kitchen, and to the back of the room he could see three doors. Each leading to what he presumed would be bedrooms or bathrooms.

Bodie moved to one of the doors while Oliver crossed to the kitchen.

He scanned a bedroom before moving into the adjoining bathroom. Yep. Someone had definitely been here, and they'd been here recently. The evidence was subtle. The odd droplet of water. The absence of dust or cobwebs.

Bending down, he saw a single black hair on the floor.

The only question: was the person or people who'd been here the men they were looking for?

Bodie was straightening when a noise made his head shoot up.

A footstep. It came from outside the house. Followed by another.

Moving quickly, Bodie pulled the gun from his ankle holster and moved to the corner of the living room. Oliver crouched behind the kitchen counter, his own weapon firmly in hand.

Two heartbeats.

Bodie slowed his breathing and let years of training take over.

That's when the window beside him shattered and a man jumped through. At the same time, the front door was smashed in and a second person entered.

Bodie aimed the gun and shot. The man was on the ground in milliseconds, narrowly missing the bullet—and exposing his speed.

The gun was kicked from Bodie's hand before he had time to shoot again, the man throwing a punch. He crouched quickly, the fist only grazing his jaw.

Kicking out his leg, Bodie sent the man to his back. He dove on top of him, throwing a punch to the man's temple.

The guy barely reacted, jabbing Bodie in the gut and flipping their bodies around.

Bodie let out a grunt.

Another punch hit him in the face, hard and fast. The pain was instant. Bodie absorbed it, focusing on the next attack. When the man's fist came at him again, Bodie had time to dodge.

He didn't. He caught the fist and twisted.

The sound of bones snapping echoed throughout the room.

This time, the man *did* react. He grabbed his wrist and howled. Bodie used the man's moment of pain to his benefit. Flipping their bodies again before grabbing the man's head and slamming it to the ground. He did it a second time. Then a third.

Blood coated the floor.

Bodie grabbed him by the throat. The asshole shot his uninjured arm forward, hitting him in the gut. Bodie didn't loosen his hold. Instead, he tightened his fingers. Watched as panic and desperation flashed through the guy's eyes.

Bodie shot a quick glance at Oliver, noticing his teammate had the other guy pushed to the wall. They'd get their information from Oliver's man.

Which meant this guy was no longer needed.

Bodie quickly grabbed the man's head and snapped his neck.

He went limp beneath him.

Standing, he moved to Oliver, lifting the gun that had been kicked to the floor on his way.

The guy Oliver secured had a knife wound to his gut, blood

dripping from the wound. It was probably the only reason Oliver could restrain him.

Oliver grabbed one of the man's wrists and pressed it against the wall. Bodie lifted the gun, placing the muzzle to the man's hand.

"I'm going to ask you some questions, and every time you lie to me, I'm going to put a hole in your body. Do you understand?"

The man struggled against Oliver's hold. "Fuck off."

Bodie pressed the gun harder to his skin. "I'm going to start with your hand. Next will be your feet. The worst will be your knees. Do you know what it feels like to have your kneecap shattered? I hear it's a pain that burns through the body like fire."

The man's breathing quickened. "Okay! What do you want to know?"

"Where's Sinclair?"

"I don't know."

Bodie took note of the man's tone as he spoke, as well as his heartbeat. He was scared, but he wasn't lying.

"After he ran into you at the fair, he wanted us to split up. Him, Jordy, and Casper went to another location. Mick and I stayed here. Sinclair was going to contact us with our next mission."

More truths.

"Sinclair has six men. If he has two with him, and you guys are here, where are the last two?"

"They were killed in Tyler."

Tyler. That's where Wyatt had gone with Quinn to pick up Maya. Only Maya hadn't been there. Instead, two men had broken into the apartment and attacked, and Wyatt killed them.

Sinclair's men.

"How did Sinclair get involved in Project Arma?" Oliver's voice was low and deadly.

"He's more than involved. Him and Hylar orchestrated the whole fucking thing."

Bodie's limbs went cold. "That's not true."

They would have uncovered that information.

"It is! The two of them served together. Known each other for years. When Project Arma started, they wiped Sinclair's past. Made it seem like they'd never met. Even changed his name in his military records so they could never be connected."

Bodie shot a look to Oliver. His friend had the same expression of shock and disbelief on his face. Hylar had told them *he'd* created the project. He'd never mentioned a partner.

And to wipe someone's past...that required a whole lot of power.

"What were they hoping to achieve with Project Arma?"

"I don't know." Oliver pulled the man's head off the wall before brutally shoving it back. The guy grunted before raising his voice. "I'm telling the truth! I don't know! I worked for Sinclair. He let me and five other guys in on the project. He took us to the facility before it shut down, gave us drugs to make us stronger and faster. He didn't tell us *everything*."

Shit. The guy still wasn't lying.

"What does he want with Maya?"

The guy's breathing was labored, but not nearly as bad as moments ago. "Fuck. You."

Wrong answer.

Bodie was about to pull the trigger when the guy shoved back against Oliver, hard enough to cause him to stumble, then kicked out at Bodie, making him stagger a few feet backward.

The man reached for his ankle, presumably for a holstered weapon.

Bodie shot him in the head before he'd even pulled it out.

CHAPTER 23

*M*aya's eyes popped open at the sound of voices. Hushed voices coming from the living room.

Bodie, Oliver, and Wyatt.

Glancing at the clock, she noticed it was almost four in the morning. Bodie had fallen asleep with her, but she'd known before they'd headed to bed that he'd be leaving at some point in the night to check out a location in the hopes of finding Sinclair.

The voices in the other room continued but were too quiet to understand. She should go back to sleep. After all, Bodie would tell her everything she needed to know in the morning.

Her eyes had only been closed for a second before they shot back open.

Nope. She couldn't sleep. Not while the guys were out there, possibly discussing whether or not they'd caught Sinclair.

Creeping out of bed, Maya moved to the bedroom door. It was cracked open. A sliver of light poked through. Standing as close to the opening as possible, she could just hear the conversation.

"You have to have a lot of power to change military records," Oliver said quietly.

There was light tapping of a keyboard before Wyatt spoke. "Being an agent in the CIA, he would have had lots of connections. Connections to people who could be bought to do just about anything."

"He was our commander for years," Bodie sighed, "yet he never mentioned his SEAL team from when he'd served. That alone should have been a red flag for us."

More typing.

"Maya."

A squeal escaped Maya's lips and she jumped backward at Bodie's voice. His *close* voice. So much closer than it had been a second earlier.

Nibbling her lip, she slowly pulled the door open to find Bodie exactly where she thought he was…less than a foot away.

Crap. He must have heard her get up. Actually, now that she thought about it, of course he did. The man had super hearing. A fact she needed to remember. He probably knew the moment she woke. She expected him to ask her why she was eavesdropping. Maybe give her a disapproving look. Something to illustrate his annoyance.

He didn't. Instead, Bodie reached out his hand and laced his fingers through hers, leading her to the couch. He dropped down before pulling her onto his lap.

Maya relaxed against him. Loving that he trusted her enough to be part of this conversation.

Wyatt sat on the other end of the sofa, computer on his lap and focused expression on his face. Oliver stood across the room, staring at the floor, his arms folded.

She was about to look away when she noticed Oliver's torn black shirt. There were two tears, one on the left shoulder and another on the bottom.

There were also specks of blood splattered across his arms and neck.

Immediately, Maya turned to study Bodie. He also wore a

black shirt and jeans but there were no tears or blood. There was a light bruise across his cheek bone from where someone had clearly hit him.

Lifting her hand, Maya trailed her fingers across his cheek. "Are you okay?"

A small smile stretched his lips. "I'm okay. We didn't find Sinclair tonight, but we ran into a couple of his men. We got crumbs of information. We're going to see if we can build on it."

Crumbs were better than no information. "What did you learn?"

"That Hylar didn't establish Project Arma alone." Bodie paused, the thumb of the hand on her waist sneaking beneath her shirt to stroke her skin. "Sinclair and Hylar were equally responsible for Project Arma."

Whoa. That was a big crumb. "And you guys had no idea."

It was more a statement than a question. She knew they had no idea. That until Maya had confirmed Sinclair's involvement in the project, they'd only had suspicions.

"We assumed Sinclair was probably paid to protect Hylar and his organization." That was a fair assumption. "We also found out Hylar and Sinclair served in the military together."

"Got him."

Bodie's thumb stilled on her waist as everyone's attention shot to Wyatt.

He turned the laptop around to reveal an image of eight men. They wore military attire with weapons strapped to their bodies.

Wyatt pointed to a man in the middle. "Hylar." He shifted his finger to the man beside him. "And Sinclair. With the rest of their SEAL team."

Maya worked hard to suppress the sliver of fear threatening to course down her spine at the sight of a younger-looking Sinclair. He looked happy. They all did.

Wyatt spun the laptop back around. "I hacked the US military files. Now that I know what to look for, it's a hell of a lot easier."

He pressed more keys, studying the screen in front of him. "There are some reports here."

The room remained silent.

A few seconds later, Wyatt frowned before madly typing again. Then he blew out a long breath.

Oliver stepped forward. "What is it?"

"I found a report of Hylar's final mission. It didn't look right to me, so I dug a bit deeper, and I found the original."

"The original?" Bodie asked.

"I think someone rewrote it and tried to hide the original from anyone who might come looking. Unfortunately for them, most things that have been online can be found if a person looks deep enough."

"What does the original report say?" Oliver asked.

Wyatt scanned the information. Every second that passed felt heavier. Maya could tell that it wasn't good news by the expression on his face.

"The team was sent to South Sudan to extract some of the country's political leaders who'd been taken hostage." Wyatt scrubbed a hand over his face. "Something went wrong. The team was captured. The military took a long time to send help. Months. By the time help arrived, Hylar and Sinclair were the only team members still alive."

Oliver swore under his breath while Bodie stiffened.

Maya just sat there, unsure what to think or say. Movie scenes where people had been captured and tortured flashed through her mind. They must have gone through hell. And possibly had to watch their teammates be murdered. She couldn't even imagine the pain.

"Sounds like a damn good reason to hate your country," Oliver said quietly.

Bodie nodded. "Enough to build an army to use against it."

MAYA STEPPED INTO THE BATHROOM. She hadn't gone for her run today. Bodie had flat-out refused to let her, while Quinn had threatened to barricade the door with her body.

She knew they were right. Hell, she'd passed out yesterday, she should be in bed resting.

Then why did the fact that she couldn't run make her feel so damn upset?

She knew the answer to that. Because, until now, she'd refused to let her heart be just one more thing to have power over her...and now it was.

Maya had grown so used to using runs to forget her problems. She needed that escape this morning. Needed to forget Sinclair's voice. Needed a break from the knowledge that she needed the surgery sooner rather than later but had no means to afford it.

Closing the door, she stood at the mirror. She saw everything in her reflection. All the emotions. The exhaustion. The uncertainty about the future.

The only thing that was keeping her going was the discovery that she loved Bodie. The very fact that he hadn't let her run this morning, that he'd protected her from herself, just confirmed it further.

Love. Even the word in her head made her want to gulp down giant breaths of air.

He was the first man she'd ever loved. And what was more, she trusted him with her heart. Trusted that her feelings were reciprocated. She'd lived thirty-three years not knowing that this kind of connection existed. A connection that drew you to another person's soul in such an intimate way.

The tough part would be saying the words out loud. She could speak them in her head, but wasn't sure if she was at the stage of saying them to Bodie yet.

Dropping her chin, Maya took some deep breaths. Her chest

was still tight. Bodie and Quinn had been right, of course. She had to accept that running was beyond her right now.

Stripping off her clothes, she stepped into the shower. Closing her eyes, she worked on taking deep breaths.

A knock on the door had Maya's head lifting.

"Can I come in?"

When she was quiet for a bit too long, Bodie spoke again. "Maya?"

"Uh…sure."

She expected Bodie to talk to her from *outside* the shower. She was surprised when he stepped inside the bathroom, stripped naked, and got under the spray with her.

The man took up all the space in the best kind of way. The heat radiating from his body almost felt hotter than the water.

Bodie placed gentle hands on her waist. "Deep breaths with me. In," they both took a long, slow breath in, "out." Then slowly exhaled.

They repeated that over and over again, Maya's eyes never leaving Bodie's.

This was the third time Bodie had asked her to breathe with him. Each time, her chest felt that much better after.

"Tell me about your heart," Bodie said, eventually.

"What do you want to know?" She *knew* what he wanted to know. But she was nervous to tell him the truth. That she needed surgery but wouldn't be getting it. At least, not for the moment.

Bodie's hands tightened, and he lifted her body against his. Her legs immediately wrapped around his waist. The hold was intimate. Her blood warmed at their touch.

"Do you need surgery?"

Crunch time. "Yes. I was booked for surgery. I was supposed to have it a week after the lab break-in. But I left New York."

Not just left. Ran away and disappeared. Hid until Bodie found her.

Concern flickered across his face. "What happens if you don't have the surgery soon?"

There was no point in lying. "I'm at risk of developing other heart, lung, and blood problems. Serious problems."

This time, a myriad of emotions passed over his face. Worry. Frustration. Anger. Even sadness. "We're booking the surgery today."

If only it was that simple. "I had good health insurance when I worked for Novac Pharmaceuticals. I no longer work there, so I no longer have insurance. I don't have the means to pay for it." Surgery without insurance was beyond expensive. She ran her fingers across Bodie's wet shoulder before she continued. "My plan was, when I felt safe enough, I would try to negotiate a payment plan with a hospital."

Although, to be honest, she hadn't put too much thought into it because she'd questioned whether she would *ever* feel safe enough.

"I've got money, Maya. You're having the surgery."

Bodie had *his* money. She couldn't let him pay for such an expensive operation. She had no idea when she would be able to pay him back. "We haven't been seeing each other that long."

"Guess I fell for you fast then."

Her eyes widened. "Fell for me...?"

"You're right. I should say it properly. I love you, Maya." Her breath hitched at his words. "I don't expect you to say it back, I just need you to know that's how I feel. I love your smile. Your sweet nature. I love that you treat customers at the bar— complete strangers—like you have all the time in the world for them. I love you."

She opened and closed her mouth a couple of times before she was able to make her voice work. Her heart was working overtime, so too was her brain. "No one's ever loved me before."

Saying those words out loud again hurt. She'd always felt

them, always been affected by them, but never voiced them before Bodie.

Bodie pushed a lock of hair behind her ear. "That makes me unbelievably sad and angry. You deserve better, Maya. You deserve so much love. I hope I can even partly make it up to you. I want to make you feel as special as you are."

God, what had she done to deserve this man? His words, his touch...they almost made her heart feel whole.

"Thank you." She moved her hands to his neck. "I'm sorry I'm not ready to say it back yet." She hoped she would be ready soon.

Bodie didn't appear annoyed in the slightest. "You don't need to say sorry for anything. Part of loving someone is being patient." He lowered his head and touched his lip to hers.

Emotions stirred up in her chest. Warmth. Appreciation.

Love.

CHAPTER 24

*B*odie shoved his phone in his pocket and headed back down the hall toward his apartment. Maya was booked into the Marble Falls Hospital to get the surgery she needed in one week. Usually, it wouldn't be so easy. Luckily, they had Sage on their team, and she had connections.

If it was up to him, she'd be booked in sooner. Today, even. As it was, a week was the soonest they could make it.

Tomorrow, they were working their final shifts at the bar before heading to Marble Falls. He hated that he was rushing Maya. He wanted her to make the decision to join him in her own time. Unfortunately, the severity of her heart condition meant that instead of wanting to go back for his team, he *needed* to go back for her health. She needed the surgery, and soon.

Marble Falls would be the safest place for the procedure. His entire team was there. There was safety in numbers.

Stepping inside his apartment, his attention was immediately drawn to Maya's laugh. The sound floated from the kitchen to the door. Maya was busy preparing breakfast with Quinn and Oliver while Wyatt worked in the spare bedroom, trying to locate Sinclair.

"Here's the big guy. You can ask him yourself." Oliver chuckled as he turned to the stove.

Maya smiled over at Bodie like she knew a secret she shouldn't. "Oliver told me the guys call you Red."

That was true. It definitely wasn't the reason for the look on her face though. "They do."

"Will you tell me the story behind the name?"

There was a very real possibility Oliver already had, but hell, he didn't care. Where most of the team had nicknames linked to their speed or strength or something heroic that they'd done, Bodie didn't.

"Sure." He stepped up to the kitchen counter, popping a piece of strawberry into his mouth. "We completed a mission in Paris. It had been pure hell, and we were all exhausted. I was sharing a room with Oliver, who'd invited a woman up for a drink. I was so tired, I crashed. Woke up the next morning with red polish on my finger and toenails."

Oliver snickered at the stove, knowing how this story ended.

"I think that would have looked nice," Quinn said from her place at the counter, cutting up more fruit.

"We were supposed to leave the next morning," Bodie continued. "Unfortunately, we woke to find our mission had been extended. It wasn't quite as finished as we'd thought. I completed the operation with red nails."

Quinn threw her head back and laughed, whereas Maya seemed to be trying to hold hers in.

Oliver smirked. "I swear his red nails are what distracted the bad guys long enough to give us the advantage. Good damn luck, they were."

Bodie lifted a shoulder. "None of it bothered me. I'm very comfortable with my masculinity."

Maya's smile broadened. "Red nails, blue nails...you'd look good with any color."

Rounding the corner, Bodie snaked his arms around her

waist, loving the soft sigh that escaped her lips. "You can paint my nails anytime you want." Heck, she could paint his nails the colors of the rainbow if it made her happy. He nuzzled her neck. "Mm, everything in here smells good." Mostly the woman in his arms. Food was an afterthought.

"Good, because it's ready." Oliver transferred a pancake from the pan to a tray that was already overflowing with them.

The four of them worked together to set the table and put the food in the middle. Quinn even managed to wrangle Wyatt out of work mode to join them. Although, when the man came out, he looked more frustrated than ever.

Damn. That had to mean no location for Sinclair. At least, not yet.

Conversation remained light throughout breakfast. Maya seemed very interested to hear every detail about Bodie's life that his friends were willing to share, which was a lot. She learned that his favorite food was pasta—any and all pasta—his most embarrassing moment was when he'd fallen asleep on the toilet while drunk at a high school party and that the episode was the reason he absolutely did not remain friends with anyone from school.

They also mentioned Luca's upcoming wedding.

"Your friend's getting married?" Maya looked both excited and surprised about the prospect. Probably surprised because who plans a wedding when they're in the middle of hunting a deadly enemy.

Oliver forked a piece of pancake off his plate. "Yep. It will be small. Us and his immediate family."

"When?"

Bodie was sure if it was up to Luca, the wedding would be today. But the man also wanted Evie to have a semblance of normalcy. To be able to plan the day. Choose her flowers. Find her dress.

Wyatt lifted his coffee to his lips. "They haven't chosen a date yet."

Quinn nodded. "Most women spend years planning their wedding. Luckily, Evie's not high-maintenance so it probably won't take her that long."

Oliver leaned back in his seat. "What a waste of money. Why can't people just be together without needing to pay thousands of dollars to stand in front of a crowd and say I love you?"

Quinn huffed, but Maya spoke before the other woman could.

"I think it's about the declaration of love," she said quietly. "A man standing in front of all of his loved ones and promising that he'll always love you. Telling you all the reasons why." Maya shrugged. "Sounds pretty special to me."

Ah, hell. If that didn't make him want to marry the woman, nothing would.

Bodie reached for her hand and lifted it to his lips. "That's exactly what it's about."

Maya didn't need to say the words out loud for him to know that she cared about him. He didn't mind one bit that he'd professed his love for her and she hadn't reciprocated. It would take her a little more time than it took him. Progress was progress.

"I agree," Quinn said, appearing a bit less annoyed than a moment ago. "When I marry a man, he's going to declare that he loves me in front of hundreds of people."

Wyatt's brows drew together. "Hundreds?"

"Yep."

Bodie had to chuckle at the unrelenting look on Quinn's face.

Maya's fingers tightened around his. "What's in the cards for today?"

"I think some of your things are still at the house." Bodie pressed a kiss to her head, for no other reason than because he wanted to. "We could go pack them before work."

"We'll come. I'll help you pack your room. Girl time." Quinn winked at Maya.

Bodie smiled. "Girl time" would have to mean the men were still present, just in a different room.

❧

QUINN HADN'T BEEN LYING about wanting girl time. The moment Wyatt and Bodie stepped outside to do a perimeter check, she grabbed Maya's arm and pulled her into the bedroom, firmly closing the door after them.

When she pushed Maya toward the bed, she went along with it. Packing wouldn't take long, after all; she'd arrived in town with barely anything.

"Okay, tell me. Is it official?" Quinn looked far too excited.

"Official?" Did official mean they'd used the "girlfriend and boyfriend" tags, or could it just mean he'd said he loved her?

Quinn rolled her eyes, obviously all too aware of Maya's avoidance tactic. "Is Bodie your boyfriend?"

Was he? Probably. "I think so."

At the sight of Quinn's frown, Maya knew that hadn't been the answer she was looking for. "What do you mean, 'you think so'? You're moving to Marble Falls with the guy."

That was true. Although that decision had basically been made for her.

Maya bit her lip as she debated what to say to Quinn. They hadn't known each other for a huge amount of time, but Maya already felt close to the other woman. She was easy to feel comfortable around. In fact, if Maya wasn't careful, she would spill her guts.

"You're going to think I'm silly." Or weak. Or just downright pathetic.

Quinn took Maya's hand and held it in hers. "Spill."

She kept her voice low as she spoke. Oliver was inside, so he

190

would definitely hear. Hopefully Bodie was far enough away that he wouldn't.

"I want to tell Bodie how I feel." She really, really wanted to. "But, I feel this paralyzing fear. Like once the words are out there, in the ether, something will go horribly wrong."

God, that sounded even more stupid out loud than it had in her head.

Quinn leaned forward. "That's normal. Sharing your feelings with another person *is* scary. You're making yourself vulnerable."

Vulnerable. That's exactly how she felt.

"He's told me how he feels, so it's not like I have anything to lose." Actually, she probably had more to lose if she *didn't* tell him.

"But you feel like you do have something to lose."

Yes. Absolutely, yes. Maya nodded.

"Why?"

Maya lifted a shoulder. "There are so many moments in my childhood that have scarred my heart."

"Tell me one."

Maya swallowed. "When I was twelve, I was placed with the Jenkins family. They were this perfect nuclear family who actually seemed to like me." *And want to keep me.* "I was so young, but I still remember thinking—this is it. I've finally found my people."

Silly. History should have taught her better.

"I stayed with them for six months before they told me they needed to focus on *their* kids. They wished me well and waved goodbye as my case worker drove me away."

The next place had been far less homey.

"Oh, jeez. I'm so sorry, Maya. That must have been hard."

She lifted a shoulder and played it off like it wasn't one of the defining moments of her life. "I was temporary for them. Just like I've been temporary for every other person. It's hard for me to trust that anyone may want me forever."

So admitting her love for Bodie, telling him she wanted them to be together forever, felt like it was daring the universe to prove her wrong. Her chest constricted. She took some deep breaths in an attempt to keep her emotions in check.

Quinn's hand tightened around Maya's. The woman looked both angry and upset. "That family lost so much by letting you go. Every family did. I have no idea what the future holds for you guys. But I promise you that admitting you love someone, especially someone who adores you the way Bodie does, saying the words aloud for the world to hear, can never be wrong. Ever. Scary? Yes. Exposed to the point you want to hide behind a big old rock? Absolutely. But not wrong. And not something you should ever regret."

There was so much certainty in Quinn's voice. It was impossible not to trust her.

She didn't need to ignore her fear or push it aside. She needed to breathe through it, like she had every obstacle in her life. She needed to remember that the fear was a sign of how important something is. How important Bodie is.

"You're right."

A wide smile spread across Quinn's face. "Hell yes, I'm right."

Maya laughed. The woman was like medicine for the soul.

Quinn chuckled. "Aren't you glad you met me?"

She really, really was.

"I'm so glad I met you. Thank you. For reaching out to me and not giving up."

Before Maya could anticipate it, Quinn pulled her into a hug. Maya would never grow tired of a Quinn hug. So tight and affectionate.

"I'm thankful, too."

Maya wrapped her own arms around her, her heart warming.

CHAPTER 25

"*I*sn't it supposed to be my job to surprise you?"

Maya didn't let go of Bodie's hand. She just kept tugging him down the street.

Later tonight, they were working their final shift at the bar. It was also their final night in Keystone. So she wanted today to be special. She didn't want it to be about Sinclair or her heart. She just wanted it to be about her and Bodie.

Oliver, Wyatt, and Quinn were remaining close—like, restaurant-across-the-street close—so that she and Bodie could have a final date before they left.

"Why? Because you're a man? Bodie, we live in a modern society. Those gender roles have no place here." Not that she would complain if he organized the next romantic date for her...or the next fifty.

As they drew closer to the bar, Bodie gave her a skeptical look. "You taking me to work, woman? When I said let's not be late for our final shift, I didn't mean let's arrive three hours early."

Maya chuckled. She didn't need reminding of how long they had before their shift. She'd planned this date to sit perfectly between lunch and dinner. Trish usually remained open in between, but every so often she closed the bar for a few hours. Luckily, that's exactly what she'd done today.

It might have had something to do with Maya's begging.

When they stopped in front of the bar, she took the key from her pocket and unlocked the door.

Bodie was looking more suspicious by the second. "Did you rob Trish for her key? Am I going to have to protect you from her too?"

"I did," Maya said, pushing the door open. "I tackled the woman to the ground, wrenched the key from her fingers and told her if she disturbed our midafternoon date, she'd be in trouble."

And if the guy believed that, he didn't know either woman at all. Trish was tough. Maya was sure if she even attempted to steal anything from her boss, she'd end up seriously injured.

Bodie chuckled as they stepped inside. The bowls of pasta and glasses of wine were sitting exactly where she'd asked Trish to leave them. Maya had organized for them to be delivered from a local Italian restaurant fifteen minutes ago, coinciding with when Trish was leaving. Trish had also set the table for them, bless her soul.

Maya looked up to see one side of Bodie's mouth lift. It made the dimple in his cheek stand out. Sigh. She'd never tire of seeing his dimples.

"You organized this?"

She lifted a shoulder. "This place is special because it's where we first met. I actually asked Trish to put the food on that table specifically, because it's the closest to where you helped me clean up the broken glasses." Pink tinged her cheeks. It sounded silly when she said it out loud. Maybe she should have kept that tidbit to herself.

Bodie swept his arms around her, pulling her against his chest. "God, I love you."

Heat rushed through her chest at his words.

I love you, too.

She wanted to say it back to him. The words were right there on the tip of her tongue, but when her mouth opened, nothing came out.

Bodie dipped his head and kissed her. A long, sweet kiss that had her chest humming.

When he finally drew away, she was short on breath, but her heart was full.

Bodie moved to the table and pulled out her chair. Anyone watching would think that he was the one taking *her* on a date. He took a look at his bowl as he sat across from her. "Is this pesto pasta?"

"Maybe. Do you like pesto pasta?"

"It's only the greatest combination of foods on earth. So yeah, I like it, sweetheart. Thank you."

Maya couldn't take all the credit. Oliver may have mentioned that Bodie liked pesto. Combine that with Bodie saying his favorite food was pasta, and there it was.

"I just put the request in. The guys at the Italian place down the street did all the work."

"You're amazing. Thank you. I don't know what I did to deserve this, to deserve *you*, but I'm a lucky man."

Her cheeks flushed at his words. The man was so easy to like. It was a wonder no woman had snapped him off the market before her. She took a bite of her food but was more focused on the sheer pleasure that crossed Bodie's face. He looked happy. And peaceful. It made *her* feel happy and peaceful.

"God, I love pasta," he said, probably not realizing she could tell just by watching him. "When we were on active duty, I would go weeks without the stuff. It was hell. I kid you not, I would dream about it."

Maya laughed. She didn't think she'd ever dreamed about

pasta, but then, she obviously didn't have the same level of appreciation as Bodie. "Was it just pesto pasta you dreamed about?"

"Nope. I mean, yes, I dreamed about pesto pasta. But also lasagna. Carbonara. Oh, and my mom makes a killer chicken fettuccini. I don't even know what she puts in the thing to make it so good, I just know that I would do many, many terrible things to get my hands on the stuff."

She wasn't sure she believed that for a second. "From everything I've learned about you, you don't seem capable of doing terrible things."

Some of the joy slipped from Bodie's face. Maya immediately wanted to take her words back.

"As a SEAL, I've needed to do some terrible things. Always to bad people—scum-of-the-Earth type people—but still, terrible things."

On instinct, Maya reached across the table and touched his hand. He immediately threaded his fingers through hers.

"I'm sure by doing those 'terrible things,' you saved others. Probably many." Bodie's silence confirmed her suspicions. "You're a hero, Bodie. The world needs more people like you in it." Some of the tension dropped from his features. Maya almost breathed a sigh of relief.

"More sexy men with pasta addictions?"

She laughed, the final bit of tension easing from her body. "Yes. That is exactly what the world needs. Lots and lots of you."

"Sorry, ma'am. I'm a one of a kind. An original. Luckily for you though, I'm yours."

She felt the tightening of his fingers around her hand. "Guess that *does* make me one lucky woman."

She wasn't even joking. Not one bit. His gaze heated before she gently pulled away.

Bodie went on to tell her stories about his other friends back home. He told her about a man the team called Hunter, who stood at six feet six. Hunter had pulled the short straw on a mission and had to crawl through ceiling air vents.

Another guy called Cage, a ladies' man, once got robbed by a woman he'd taken back to his hotel room. His phone, wallet, and plane ticket were stolen, almost resulting in him not getting home.

Some of the stories were funny. Some were downright scary. Like when his team had to fight a group of terrorists on a cliff edge, and both he and Oliver almost fell thirty feet.

"I can't even begin to imagine some of the moments that you've lived through." *That you've survived.*

Bodie lifted a shoulder like it was no big deal. "We were well-trained for that stuff. Things didn't always go to plan, but we always had each other to watch our backs."

"I'm excited to meet the rest of your team."

Also nervous. Very nervous. She could tell the men meant a lot to Bodie. He'd referred to them as brothers on numerous occasions. That meant it would be important to him that they liked her.

As if reading her thoughts, Bodie leaned forward. "I can't wait either. They're going to love you."

When the music changed to "Your Song" by Elton John, Maya closed her eyes. "Oh, I love this song. It was when I heard it sung on *Moulin Rouge* that I really fell in love with it. I've been hopelessly obsessed ever since."

Bodie stood and held out his hand. "Dance with me."

Dance with the man she loved to her favorite song? Um...yes.

Placing her hand in his, she let him pull her to the open space between the bar and the tables. His arms snaked around her waist and she moved so her body was pressed to his. He held her so closely, they were almost one.

Sighing, Maya placed her hands on his shoulders and her head to his chest.

This was it. The feeling that people chased. The one that some spent their whole lives searching for...perfection. Peace. Love. She'd found it.

If there was ever a time to tell a man she loved him, it was now.

Be fearless, Maya.

Bodie pressed a kiss to her head. "I need to tell you something. I know we agreed that you'd get your surgery in Marble Falls, but we never discussed when. Usually new doctors mean new pre-surgery appointments and wait periods. But Sage, our team doctor, has managed to work some magic and get you scheduled in for the surgery next week."

Maya lifted her head in surprise. She felt unbelievably grateful that Bodie's friend had gone to all that effort, but she didn't have the money yet.

"I know you don't want me to pay for it," he continued. "I know things are dangerous and complicated right now. But your health and safety are my priority. I can't lose you. I *won't*. So, I hope you're okay with—"

"I love you."

The last bit of fear eased from her chest. This man, with his sweet words and actions, was everything to her. He needed to know that.

When Bodie remained quiet, Maya took advantage and hurried to continue. "For a while, I thought maybe I wasn't capable of feeling love or being loved. I think I even feared it a little bit. You've taught me not to fear love, but to embrace it. That I'm deserving of both giving and receiving." She took a breath. "You're the first man I've ever loved. The only man I likely will ever love. I can't picture my life, my future, without you in it."

She'd been doing just fine surviving without him. But he made her want more than survival; he made her want to *live*.

The smile on Bodie's lips grew slowly. "You have no idea how happy that makes me. You're everything to me, Maya. You have my whole heart. Every little part of it."

Then he kissed her. And the danger, the uncertainty, a lifetime of hurt and loneliness, it all faded. Bodie took up all the space in her head and heart, leaving room for nothing else.

CHAPTER 26

"These new bartenders better be good, or I'll be keeping you and Maya here until I can find other workers."

Bodie looked up from the glass he was filling with beer to glance at Trish beside him. Behind her, he noticed Tom, one of the new bartenders, serving two women. Bodie didn't need to look across the room to know that the other newbie, Tina, was cleaning tables.

Both were well-known Keystone locals. Both in their early twenties, with no experience working in a bar.

"It wasn't long ago that Maya and I were pretty terrible at this job. If memory serves me correctly, Maya broke about two dozen glasses in the first couple weeks, I had to pour out a few drinks before I got the ratios right, and we were both slow. But look at us now? We could run the joint."

Okay, that might be a slight exaggeration, but they definitely wouldn't run the place into the ground if left alone for a few nights.

Trish laughed. "Don't get ahead of yourself. And the difference is that I knew you both had potential. I'm not too sure about these guys. They look...less efficient."

Bodie pushed the beer across the bar, taking money from the customer before turning back to Trish. "What can I say, Maya and I set a high standard. People as awesome as us don't just grow on trees." He gave Trish a wink, expecting a laugh, or at least a smile. If anything, her face became more serious.

"You've done good." Trish took a step forward and lowered her voice. "When that girl walked in here looking for a job, I felt her fear and desperation. It was like a thick fog that surrounded her. That's gone now. She's almost a different woman. I'm glad you could help her."

Bodie was glad too. He just wished *all* the danger was gone.

"It was good of you to give her a job when she so desperately needed one." Had she not, Maya may have left town, and who knew if Bodie would have been able to find her. "It was also good of you to take pity on my sad ass and let me work here. Not to mention letting Maya and I have shifts together."

Bodie had never asked for that. Trish had just scheduled them that way. The woman knew more than she let on.

She lifted a shoulder. "Like I told you when we first met, I know what it feels like to run from someone. You looked like someone who could help her." Trish finally cracked a smile. "And I could see you two were both besotted with each other. Who am I to stand in the way of love? But you'd better be coming back and visiting. Regularly."

Bodie chuckled. "Was always planning on it."

"Good." Trish gave him a final nod before stepping away to serve a customer.

Bodie searched the crowd for Maya. She was taking drinks to a table at the back, close to the one where Wyatt, Quinn, and Oliver sat. The three of them had been there since opening and would likely stay until closing.

Having his friends close by helped Bodie breathe a little easier, not knowing where Sinclair and his remaining men were. Had it still been just him in town, he would have fought tooth and nail to ensure Maya's safety, but having his team there took some of the pressure off.

The next hour passed quickly. The bar filled and Bodie found his focus taken up with getting drinks out.

"You taking that girl away from here, boy?"

Bodie stopped in front of Roe, who sat in the same spot where he'd been sitting since Bodie's first shift. Without needing to be asked, Bodie grabbed his usual beer.

"Yes, sir, I am. Taking her to meet the rest of my team. Men who are also my family."

Roe pressed his lips together, making himself look every bit the former law enforcement officer he'd once been. "She deserves a man who's gonna look after her. You that man?"

Bodie pushed the beer across the counter. "Maya is damn strong and does a good job of taking care of herself. But when she needs extra support, I'll be there. By her side. Protecting her. She deserves the best, and I hope to be that for her."

He'd just about dedicate his life to being the best man he could for the woman.

Roe studied Bodie's face for another beat before nodding. "Good. Ain't nothing I hate more than a man not treating a woman right."

"Couldn't agree more, Roe. And anytime you find yourself around Marble Falls, pop in and check for yourself. There's a spare room at my place with your name on it."

Some of the intensity dropped as his features lightened. "There a bar in Marble Falls?"

Where the hell wasn't there a bar? "Of course."

Roe lifted the beer to his lips. "Might just take you up on that offer."

Bodie hoped he did.

Hell, he was going to miss Keystone and all its characters. Not only would he be leaving Roe and Trish, he would also be leaving the town where he'd met and fallen in love with Maya.

When there was a lull in customers, his gaze swung across the room. It had been an hour since he'd talked to her. Touched her. Kissed her.

Too damn long.

Moving around the bar, he walked right up to the woman. Without uttering a word, Bodie pulled her down the hall and into the staff room. Then he kissed her.

She didn't stop to ask questions. She just kissed him back.

Damn, but the woman shattered him. Her full lips moving on his had Bodie's heart pounding against his ribs. Her soft curves pressed close made his body ache with need.

It took a full minute before either of them could pull away. Even then, it was tough. When he looked down at her, it was to see her beautiful eyes glazed over with lust.

"Mmm, that was nice."

Bodie wouldn't call it nice. He would call it fire seeping into his bones. "I missed you."

She giggled. A soft, lyrical giggle that had him clenching his fists to stop from pulling her to him again. "You kissed me an hour ago."

He touched his lips to hers. This time softly. "I know. I counted the minutes."

And the seconds.

Her eyes heated. Then she sighed and gently pushed him away. "We need to get back out there. It's busy. And the new staff are struggling."

As if on cue, a crash sounded from the bar. It was loud enough for Maya to hear, because an "I told you so" smile touched her lips.

Reluctantly, Bodie took Maya's hand and led them out. He spotted one of the new bartenders immediately. Tina was placing the broken shards of glass on her tray. It was just about a mirror image of all those weeks ago, when Maya had dropped her own tray, and no one helped.

Bodie growled softly at the complete disregard of others. "I'll help her."

Pressing a kiss to Maya's temple, he watched as she headed to the bar. Bodie moved straight to Tina and dropped to his haunches. "Let me help."

Her gaze shot up. The look in her eyes made Bodie hesitate.

He saw fear.

He'd met her earlier that night, and he'd thought she seemed nervous then. Now, it was almost as if she were a step away from a complete breakdown. And it wasn't just the look in her eyes that had him pausing. He could hear her heart beating about a hundred miles an hour in her chest.

Bodie's brows pulled together. Reaching out a hand, he touched her arm. "Hey, are you okay?"

She opened her mouth to respond, but it seemed to take her a few tries to speak. "Yes. I, uh, I'm okay."

She certainly didn't look it. Bodie wanted to push, but Tina placed the final shard of glass on the tray and stood. She moved away without sparing him a backward glance.

Okay, that was definitely weird.

Bodie headed straight to the table his friends were sitting at, all the while keeping Maya in his sights.

"Jobs, you did a background check on the new staff, didn't you?"

Wyatt nodded. "Tom Jarvis. Dropped out of college six months ago. Lives with two friends here in Keystone. Likes to party. The woman is Tina Abalos. She also works at the local coffee shop and lives with her mother. My digging found that they may be living here illegally, but that's really none of my business. Why do you ask?"

Bodie ran a hand through his hair. "Might be nothing. The woman just seems overly nervous. Scared even."

Oliver sat a little straighter. "Could it just be first-shift nerves?"

He looked across the room to see Tina coming out of the short hall holding a box of beer. She walked behind the bar, stopped near the middle, and placed the box on the floor before going toward the back room again.

"Maybe." *Maybe not.*

Bodie sought out Maya. She stood at the end of the bar, near the hall, talking to Roe and laughing at something he said.

Suddenly, his gut clenched. He had no idea why. A sick feeling told him to go to her.

Bodie had taken a step in that direction when a loud explosion roared through the room.

The force of the blast threw Bodie backward, his body hitting a table. He didn't stay down for long. He was on his feet within seconds.

Chaos surrounded him. Smoke clouded the room, and fire billowed from the center of the bar. People were running around screaming while others lay injured or motionless on the floor.

Icy panic clawed its way up his throat. He needed to find Maya.

Bodie moved across the room to the last place he'd seen her. He searched the cluttered floor. She wasn't there.

Fuck. Where was she?

His panic turned to fear. There was an exit in the storage room. If someone had taken her, that's where they'd go.

Running down the hall, he pushed through the back door and stepped outside just in time to see a man shoving Maya into the back seat of a four-door pickup truck. The man jumped in the front and the truck started moving down the street—fast.

Terror stabbing at his chest, Bodie took off after it. He'd never tested his speed before. He could only hope that he was as fast as a speeding truck, or at least fast enough to keep it within his sights.

His friends would be able to track him through the GPS on

his phone. Bodie's job was to keep up with the truck. Wyatt or Oliver would need to find a car and follow. Hopefully, a fast one.

The truck wasn't built for speed. That was something in Bodie's favor.

He couldn't let Maya out of his sight. It wasn't an option.

Bodie ran as fast as his body allowed, keeping pace with the truck...just. People might see how fast he was moving. Notice he wasn't normal.

None of that mattered. Maya's safety was his only priority.

He saw the gun poke out the passenger window before any shots were fired.

Bodie dodged the first bullet. Then the next. Each time, it cost him precious distance.

When the truck turned a corner, then another, Bodie almost lost them. He had to push himself, push his body, to the absolute limit to catch up.

A car sounded from behind him. He didn't take his eyes off the truck. A couple of seconds later, the car caught up, and a passenger door opened.

Bodie threw his body inside the vehicle. In the process, Oliver had to slow down enough to put distance between them and the truck. The moment the door was shut, Oliver pressed his foot to the gas pedal.

"You okay?"

Bodie wasn't so much as breathing heavily. But that in no way made him okay. "I'm ready to murder the assholes."

CHAPTER 27

*M*aya gritted her teeth as she was thrown into the door of the truck. Two large men sat in the front, one of which had been the person to yank her from the bar when the explosion went off.

She hadn't had time to panic in the bar. Everything had happened so quickly. Her last thought before being thrown into the back seat was of Bodie…God, she hoped he was okay. That his friends were okay, and Roe and Trish and Shayna.

Maya breathed long, slow breaths to try to calm the panic.

The thing that had her freaking out the most was the man who sat on the other side of the back seat. The man who'd been a constant in her nightmares for the last few months.

Sinclair. She wanted to put as much distance between them as possible, but every time her body was thrown to the left, she just about fell into him.

"Faster. They're catching up." Sinclair's voice was edged with panic.

Some of Maya's fear had eased the moment Bodie climbed into the car behind them. Watching the man she loved get shot at…the only word she could use to describe it was terrifying. Her safety was secondary to his.

Just because Bodie had jumped in the car didn't mean the thug had stopped shooting at him. The bullets continued to fly. When they'd received return fire, the shooter had quickly retreated back inside.

Maya swallowed. What the hell was the plan? It didn't look like these guys were going to be able to outdrive them, but at the same time, no one was slowing.

Glancing over her shoulder again, she could see the car was right there. She wished she could see Bodie's face, but the tinted windows made it impossible.

They were now speeding down an empty back road. There were no other cars in sight and not a single person around.

As they took a hard left turn, Maya's body hit the door again. Pain radiated down her right shoulder.

Pain that she barely recognized as the truck began to slide across the icy road.

The man behind the wheel cursed loudly as he spun the steering wheel, attempting to gain control of the vehicle.

He couldn't.

Maya tried to scream but her chest seized when the back of the truck hit a tree. The impact caused her head to be smashed against the window, Sinclair's body falling onto hers.

Then there was stillness.

Closing her eyes, she attempted to ward off the dizziness. She noticed a ringing in her ears and could just make out the sound of doors opening. Then hands were on her body. Sinclair's hands. Shoving her out of the truck.

She stumbled, immediately falling to the ground. Sinclair yanked her to her feet, his grip so tight she could practically feel her skin bruising.

Gunfire echoed through the night. It was quickly followed by the thud of bodies colliding. Fists hitting flesh.

The truck shielded them from the battle. Sinclair's nervous breaths were loud in her ear. Was he planning to wait out the fight? Was he placing all his chips on his guys winning?

The cold muzzle of a gun against her temple had Maya's breath catching. Sinclair held the weapon with one hand and her body in front of his with the other.

Oh, Jesus. The man was going to use her as a shield.

Sinclair inched away from the truck. Maya's feet were barely working, causing Sinclair to almost drag her body.

She caught her first real glimpse of the violence. Fists flew through the air and blood splattered. Each man fought with lethal tenacity and skill.

It was terrifying.

When Bodie glanced her way, his movements slowed. Their gazes fixed for less than a second. That was all it took for his opponent to gain the upper hand and tackle Bodie from behind, sending them both to the ground.

Maya attempted to lunge forward but Sinclair easily over-powered her. She struggled against his hold, arching her back and kicking, fighting with every ounce of energy she had, all the while being dragged the remaining five feet to the car that Bodie and Oliver had vacated.

Maya screamed Bodie's name just before she was shoved into the car. Sinclair almost threw her over the center console into the passenger seat as he got in after her. She immediately went for the handle but Sinclair had a gun pointed at her before she could open it.

"Don't." His voice was low and firm as he closed his door.

Dread settled like a heavy weight in her gut. She watched Bodie through the window as they drove away. For a moment, she willed him to get the upper hand. To race to her, tear the car door off, and take her in his arms.

He didn't. He was too busy fighting for his life.

When Bodie was out of sight, Maya swallowed a whimper of despair.

He was gone. *They* were gone.

She could only hope that Bodie survived. Even if he couldn't come for her, she needed him to live.

Pressing a hand to her chest, Maya tried to steady her ragged breaths. Her heart was beating so hard it was causing pain to ricochet through her chest.

"Pull your pockets out."

Maya frowned. "My pockets?"

"Now! Empty them."

She quickly did as he said, the gun pointed at her, almost daring her to defy him. She knew what he was looking for...a phone. He wouldn't find one.

Sinclair took his eyes off the road for a moment to check. Once he was satisfied, he pressed his foot harder to the accelerator.

"You've cost me a lot, bitch."

Maya's gaze shot to Sinclair at his angry words.

"I've had those men by my side for years. You cost me two men in Tyler, and two here in Keystone. If I lose my last two soldiers, it will be *your* boy who pays."

She'd cost him? If he'd stopped sending men to kill her, they would all be alive and well! The rage in Sinclair's voice matched the sudden rise of Maya's own anger.

"Maybe you should have left me alone."

Shut up, Maya. Don't anger the man further.

But instead of getting angry, Sinclair laughed. A dry laugh that had tendrils of unease crawling up her throat. "Your fate's been sealed since New York. You were never going to walk away from this."

"Because I heard your voice and knew you were involved in the lab break-in?"

There had to be more to it than that...

"That's why I went to the hospital to kill you. My plan changed when I found out about your heart defect."

Maya's brows pulled together. "Why would my heart defect change your plans?"

Sinclair took another hard right. "Because I have the same damn defect."

A thick silence filled the air. Sinclair had an atrial septal defect…a hole in his heart? Okay. That didn't explain why he needed her.

"Well, not the same. Unlike yours, mine is inoperable." There was a thread of pain in Sinclair's voice. "Doctors described my case as 'extremely rare.' The hole can't be closed with surgery because of its size and unusual position within the heart. You know what they want me to do? Enjoy my last few months of life. Just live with it and pretend like the defect isn't killing me."

He scoffed, like the very idea was ridiculous.

Maya was still waiting for him to tell her exactly where she fit into all of this.

Sinclair shook his head as he turned left. "I'm not ready to die. Not after what they did to us. And not before we achieve what we set out to do."

She was almost too nervous to ask, but she had to. "What are you talking about?"

"Wyatt found my sad story about the military screwing me over, didn't he? Of course, he did. Once they talked to you, it was only a matter of time." Sinclair took a hard right, sending Maya into the door. "We bent over backward for them. Saving whoever they told us to save. Putting our lives on the line over and over again." The sudden fury in the man's voice had Maya too scared to speak. "Then my team gets taken—and suddenly we're the ones who need saving. And you know what they did? They left us there to die! Like our lives meant *nothing*. Do you know the torture I endured? That I watched six of my seven teammates get murdered!"

Sinclair banged his fist against the wheel, causing Maya to jolt in her seat.

"In the final weeks, I was begging them to kill me. That's probably why they didn't. They enjoyed how pathetic I'd become. How desperate I was for them to stab a knife through my chest."

There was so much torment in Sinclair's voice, Maya almost felt sorry for him. If they had met under different circumstances, she would have. "How did you get out?"

"They made a mistake. They thought we were too broken to fight. I was. Hylar wasn't. They left him unbound. You should have seen him. The man went into a murderous rage. Killing everyone."

A shiver coursed down Maya's spine at the picture Sinclair painted.

"When we got home, we vowed that the government would pay. We didn't know how, but we knew they would."

"So, you created Project Arma as a way to build an army against your country?"

"We created *weapons*. The government deserves retribution for what they allowed to happen to us." He shook his head again. "And now, everything's a mess because those *assholes* are ruining it all! I think Hylar's finally getting to the point where he realizes they need to die. I told him they needed to die from the beginning. He didn't listen to me."

Maya was struggling to keep up. "I still don't understand how I come into this?"

Sinclair breathed out a long sigh as he took another left. "I told you. I'm not ready to die. Luckily, we have a great doctor who specializes in drug experimentation at Project Arma. He may have finally worked out the exact concoction of drugs that will form a clot in the hole."

Sinclair turned onto a narrow dirt road.

"We need to test it first," Sinclair continued. "Other versions that were tested all failed."

God! Is that why she was taken? To be the next patient for some experimental drug?

He shot a look at her. The dread that had been gnawing at her insides threatened to spill over.

"We'll give you the drug. It's getting harder and harder to locate people with the condition, particularly with our dwindling resources."

Maya noticed a building at the end of the road. A small building that looked to be old. Easily a hundred years or more.

"Even if I could find someone else with the condition," Sinclair continued, "at a certain point, this became about more than just killing you. It became about beating *them*. The assholes who killed my men."

Breathe, Maya. Breathe.

It was a struggle. Especially when he was slowing the car. Pulling in front of what she now saw was an old, tiny cabin.

When the car came to a stop, Maya scanned the darkness, desperate to spot someone, *anyone* who may be able to help her.

"This place is in the middle of nowhere." Sinclair's voice was casual. Like he knew she wouldn't escape, so there was no need to be anything but calm. "Most people don't even know it exists. No one will hear you."

Sinclair stepped out of the car before coming around to her side and pulling her from the passenger seat. The moon cast a dim light over the area. Maya could only just make out the ground beneath her feet.

She tugged at her arm and screamed as loud as she could. There could be *someone* around who might hear…she had to try.

Sinclair hardly paid any attention. Just kept dragging her like she was a rag doll until they stepped into the cabin.

When the door shut behind them, Maya quickly took in the tiny space. A bed occupied most of the room, with a miniscule kitchenette to the right and a bathroom to the left. The only light came from some candles around the room. She assumed that meant there was no power.

There was also a small corner table where a man sat. An older man with a bag at his feet.

"You're late," the stranger grunted.

"The assholes got in the way. Deal with it, Doc." Sinclair shoved her onto the bed. "You bring it?"

The older man opened his bag and pulled out a vial and a syringe.

Maya's jaw dropped open. The syringe was huge. So much larger than any she'd ever seen. The needle had to be two, maybe even three inches long.

"Here? You're going to test a drug on me *here*, in this cabin?" God, was she going to die in a hundred-year-old, flea-infested hellhole and never be found? "Isn't there a lab you should take me to?"

She needed time. Time for Bodie to find her.

"There's a strong chance you won't survive." Maya blanched at Sinclair's flat words. "Every other recipient has died within minutes. We'll give you the drug and if you survive, we'll wait it out. After a few days, that asshole boyfriend of yours will assume we've left town, and it'll be easier to return to Hylar."

Every other recipient has died within minutes.

She didn't even hear what he said after that. Terror filled her veins.

"You're sure they won't find us?" the doctor asked as he pierced the sealed vial with the syringe.

"This place is off the grid. It's not even on any maps. And like I said, they'll assume we're taking her to Hylar. It would be the logical course of action."

So they were going to inject her with a possibly—probably—toxic concoction of drugs, and watch to see if it kills her.

"And if I survive?" Maya finally asked when she could get her voice to work again. "What do you ultimately plan to do with me?"

"Once we get to our facility, we'll do a scan of your chest and check that the drug has worked like we hoped. Then we'll find a way for you to be useful in our organization. If it's not working on drug creation, we can use you against Bodie."

Maya watched in alarm as the doctor tapped the syringe. Sweat began to bead on her brow.

"I'm hopeful that my latest tweaks have fixed the issues we've been having." The doctor took a step toward Maya. "Hopefully, this one will form a clot in the hole without the body treating the substance as a foreign object and attacking."

Oh sweet Jesus, no.

Sinclair nodded. "Do it."

Fresh terror reared up as Sinclair moved forward to grab her. She quickly shot out a foot, hitting him right between the legs.

When he doubled over, she put the power of her whole body behind kicking his chest.

He fell to the ground as the doctor lunged toward her.

He was too slow. She was already running. Out the door and into the dark, snowy forest behind the cabin.

Maya ignored the fear moving through her blood like wildfire. She focused on putting one foot in front of the other. On pumping her arms and running as fast as her body allowed.

Her lungs protested. Her heart thudding hard behind her ribs.

She ignored it all. She was fueled by terror. By a need to live.

CHAPTER 28

*B*odie caught the fist in his hand before kicking the man to the ground. He'd taken a step forward when, from the corner of his vision, he caught sight of Maya.

His attention went to her. It couldn't not.

Sinclair held her body against his, shielding himself from the violence.

Son of a bitch.

Rage poured through Bodie's veins. He would kill the asshole.

Before Bodie could go to her, a heavy weight hit him in the back, throwing him to the ground. He swore under his breath as he flipped them both. He attempted to rise, but the man grabbed him, knife in hand.

He sliced Bodie's thigh before aiming for his chest.

Bodie grabbed the guy's hand moments before the knife hit its mark. The sound of the car engine pierced his hearing. Bodie twisted the guys' wrist around until he heard the snap.

The man cried out and the knife went flying.

Bodie jumped to his feet as the car sped away. He took one step forward before an arm came across his neck, cutting off his air.

At the realization that he was missing his chance to catch the car, an ungodly fury washed over him.

Bodie flipped the man over his shoulder. The guy barely landed before Bodie lifted him again, throwing him against a tree. He used enough force to almost knock the guy out.

Almost.

Bodie walked toward him, rage still pouring through his veins, lifting the dropped knife on the way.

The man's eyes widened a second before Bodie plunged the knife into his chest.

Turning his head, he saw Oliver still wrestling his guy on the ground. Neither man seemed to be getting the upper hand. Bodie spotted a gun that had slid across the icy road. Lifting it, he waited until he had a clear shot before shooting the man in the knee.

The guys' hands immediately released Oliver and he cried out in pain.

Oliver held the man down while Bodie trained the gun on him. "Where did they take her?" Fury made Bodie's voice shake.

The man gasped for breath, his face distorted in pain. "Fuck you!"

Bodie shot his other knee.

He didn't have an ounce of compassion for the man who'd helped kidnap his woman. The man who now sobbed beneath Oliver.

"I'll just keep putting holes in your body until you tell me."

When the guy remained silent, Bodie was about to pull the trigger again when a car engine sounded down the road. He prepared to run into the trees, disappear—until he noticed the car speeding toward them had Wyatt behind the wheel.

The car screeched to a stop beside them. Quinn sat in the passenger seat, phone in hand. They both took in the scene before Wyatt spoke. "We've been watching the GPS movement on your phones. One of them is currently on the move."

Bodie shot his gaze to Oliver. "You left your phone in the car?"

"In the center console."

Bodie could've hugged his friend. That may just save Maya's life. A small fraction of ice thawed from his chest. Not all. Not even close. He still had to hope they got to her before she was harmed.

The man below Oliver bucked his hips, and Oliver didn't hesitate to snap his neck.

He and Bodie jumped in the car, and Wyatt pressed his foot to the accelerator.

"The tracker on Oliver's phone just stopped," Quinn said from the passenger seat.

Wyatt shot a look at the phone in her hands before his eyes went back to the road. "Where?"

"At the bottom of Independence Mountain."

"What's at the bottom of Independence Mountain?"

Quinn was already shaking her head. "According to Google Maps...nothing."

Bodie's stomach clenched. He prayed Sinclair wasn't changing vehicles. If that happened, locating Maya would be ten times harder.

"You both okay?" Wyatt looked at them through the rearview mirror. "Physically, I mean."

Neither of them had come out of the fight unscathed. A long cut ran down Bodie's left thigh, while Oliver had blood staining the shoulder of his shirt.

Oliver affirmed that he was fine, and Bodie nodded.

The pain barely registered. His entire focus was on Maya. It tore at his heart that she'd been taken right in front of him. He'd put too much distance between them at the bar. And now she was paying the price.

Dammit. His insides felt raw with pain.

"I don't understand why they took her," Oliver said quietly. "By now, he would know that she's told us about him. So it's no longer about trying to keep her quiet."

Whatever it was, Bodie would be finding out—and he'd be finding out soon.

It was another ten minutes before they arrived. Ten minutes of worrying and avoiding any thoughts of worst-case scenario.

When Bodie caught sight of an old cabin up ahead, he straightened. The car Sinclair had taken from them was sitting out front.

Bodie was out of the car before Wyatt had brought it to a stop.

He heard a heartbeat clear as day coming from inside the cabin. A thread of hoped rushed through his body as he pushed inside.

It immediately died when he saw it wasn't Maya. Instead, an older man sat on a sagging bed. Bodie was on him in seconds. Grabbing him by the shirt and shoving him against the wall. "Where is she?"

The man's eyes widened, his mouth opening and closing without speaking any words.

Bodie pulled the man forward and slammed him back into the wall.

"Tell me! Or I swear to god I'll kill you."

The man lifted a shaking finger and pointed toward the door. "She ran. He followed her—"

The guy hadn't finished speaking before Bodie was moving out the door.

He saw footprints in the snow. A smaller pair and a larger pair.

He couldn't hear them yet. There was no sound of movement at all. But the moment he did, that asshole was going to die.

~

MAYA'S LUNGS BURNED. Every breath she took caused a new round of pain in her chest. She could barely see where she was going. The only light came from the reflection of the moon.

Still, she pumped her legs as fast as they would take her. Sinclair would be well-trained, but he didn't have altered DNA. That made him human. And surely if his heart defect was as severe as he'd said, it would slow him down somewhat.

She hung on to that hope like it was a lifeline.

Snow began to fall from the sky. The cold was seeping into her bones. Freezing her limbs and slowing her steps. Still, she pushed forward. Hopefully, the snow would make it harder for the man to follow.

"Where are you, bitch?"

His shout had her legs caving beneath her, falling to the ground, her hands and knees sinking into the snow.

Breathe and move. Breathe and move.

She repeated the words in her head, using them to propel herself off the ground and ignore the voice behind her. Calling on every energy reserve she had, Maya pushed to her feet. Each step became harder as her feet sank into the snow. Her body now racked with shudders.

"You think I'm going to let you get away?"

Oh, god. He was closer. So much closer than she'd hoped.

He was going to catch her. There was no doubt in her mind.

She'd only taken three more steps when the click of the safety coming off a gun echoed through the night.

"Stop!"

Maya's feet froze. She turned slowly, already knowing what she'd see.

Sinclair stood a few yards away, gun pointed at her head. His breathing labored. Possibly as labored as hers. The man looked pale.

That must be why he'd pulled the gun. He was done chasing.

"You won't shoot me." She straightened her spine. Willing the shaking in her limbs to still. If she wanted to come out of this alive, she needed to be brave.

"That's where you're wrong, kid. I could shoot you in the foot. Or the thigh. Both would keep you still long enough to inject you." He reached into his pocket and pulled out the capped syringe. "Sorry I took so long to catch up. I had to stop and grab this."

She tried not to flinch at the sight of the needle. "You're going to do it here?"

"When you're dying, every second counts. I need to live long enough to make them feel the pain that I felt. The absolute terror." He took a step forward. The gun in his hand remained trained on her. "I'm fucking *haunted* by memories of what happened to me. Every. Day. That will not go unpunished!"

Sinclair wasn't masking any emotions. She saw everything. The hate. The pain. The fear. The man had been tortured physically. But more than that, he was still tortured mentally.

"I was going to have my DNA altered too, you know. I would have been just as strong and fast as them." He shook his head. "I waited too long. The damn facility was raided. We ran out of supplies. You see why it's so important that I don't waste time? If you survive this, maybe we'll trade *you* for the drugs they stole. But this time, we'll make sure they don't swap them out."

She took a small step back. The distance closing between them was sending waves of panic through her entire body. "I'm sorry you're in pain. But this isn't my fight!"

Was it her imagination, or was there a flash of empathy across his face? "You're right. You got stuck in the middle of a war that wasn't yours. But so did I." He took another step closer. "Life isn't fair. It's a fucking shit show. We play the cards we're dealt. I learned that the hard way."

Sinclair dropped the gun and lunged for her. She screamed as she slammed into the snow, his heavy weight landing on her. Crushing her.

Maya fought him. She clawed at the man. Scratching his face. Jabbing at his eyes.

The punch he directed to her ribs sent a flame of fire through her abdomen and had her crying out in pain. She tried to curl into a ball to protect her limbs, but Sinclair's weight made it impossible.

Before she had a chance to recover from the first strike, he punched her temple.

Maya didn't make a sound this time. Her vision blurred and she felt warm liquid running down her cheek. It was either a tear or blood. Maybe both.

Her brain felt foggy and dazed.

Almost through tunnel vision, she watched as Sinclair uncapped the syringe.

Get away from me. She wanted to yell the words...scream them. Yet she couldn't voice anything.

He tore the top of her shirt open. The buttons flew into the snow.

"This is it. This has to be it..."

His words were almost a whisper to himself. Like he was praying that the contents of the syringe would heal her, and thereby be his savior.

Oh, god. If she didn't do something, and do it fast, she wouldn't get another chance.

He placed the syringe above her heart. His head was inches from hers.

Scrunching her eyes shut, Maya took a quick breath before propelling her forehead into Sinclair's nose.

The man howled in pain as blood gushed from the wound. The syringe in his hand lifted an inch away from her chest.

"You bitch!"

She bucked her hips as he pressed the syringe to her chest again. It was impossible. He didn't move an inch.

Searing pain shot through her as the needle pierced her skin. It felt like a bee sting that went impossibly deep.

"Maya!"

Bodie's voice rang in the distance. He sounded far. Too far. He wouldn't make it.

Suddenly, a deafening bang pierced the cold forest air.

A gunshot.

Sinclair grunted above her. Something dripped onto her bare chest.

Then he was gone. Replaced by Bodie.

A loud buzzing started in her ears. She watched as his mouth opened and closed. It took her a moment to realize he was talking to her, but she couldn't hear a thing.

She was vaguely aware of Bodie pulling the syringe out of her chest. She barely felt it.

A chill seeped into her bones that had nothing to do with the snow. Her heart rate slowed and every hair on her body stood on end.

Oliver knelt beside Bodie. He was holding something. The syringe Bodie had tossed to the side.

It was empty.

Panic was a mask covering Bodie's usually serene face. Her gaze lowered to his lips, but it was no use. She still couldn't make out a single word.

The buzzing was getting louder, and her eyes were feeling heavy.

As Bodie stood, he lifted her body. She felt like a rag doll, unable to grab him. Touch him. She wished she could feel his warmth, but she couldn't. She could barely *breathe*.

She opened her mouth, wanting to remind Bodie that she loved him. That this wasn't his fault. But she was almost certain that her lips weren't moving.

He knew though. No matter what happened, he already knew that he'd taught her love could exist in her world.

The darkness in her vision steadily increased until everything went black.

CHAPTER 29

*B*odie tightened his fingers around Maya's hand. She looked small in the hospital bed. Small and still. Seeing her like this made his chest ache.

She'd been unconscious for hours. An X-ray of her chest had been taken when they'd arrived, but medical staff wouldn't tell him a damn thing. They just kept repeating the same line—that he wasn't family so they couldn't disclose any information, but *hopefully* she'd wake up soon.

That didn't cut it for Bodie. Not even close.

He wasn't going to rest on hopefully. He wanted answers— and he wanted them now.

Wyatt currently sat in the hall working at hacking the hospital files, while Oliver was seeing what physical files he could get his hands on without being noticed.

Christ, this was a mess. The only small positive was that while he and Oliver had searched for Maya and Sinclair, Wyatt had remained with the doctor in the cabin. Forced the asshole to list the contents of the syringe. Every ingredient, including quantities.

When Wyatt applied some extra pressure, the doctor also

disclosed the parts of the story that had been missing. About Sinclair's heart condition. About him arriving at the New York hospital all those weeks ago with the intention of killing Maya, only to change plans when he discovered her heart defect.

But it was the knowledge that Sinclair and his six men were the only ones from the CIA working with Hylar that had them all feeling just slightly calmer. Like Bodie, Wyatt could spot when a man was lying. The doctor hadn't been.

Once Wyatt had acquired all the information they needed, he'd gotten rid of the guy, making sure no one would find the body. No one felt a second of guilt over it. The man had admitted to killing people with his drug experiments. The world was a better place without him in it.

Bodie dipped his chin to his chest, closed his eyes, and listened to Maya's heartbeat. It was the only thing keeping him sane. He needed her to be okay. To open her eyes and look at him.

As if she'd heard his thoughts, Maya's breathing changed. It shifted from long, deep breaths, to short, erratic ones. At the same time, the soft pitter-patter of her heart sped up a notch and her hand beneath his twitched.

Maya was waking.

Bodie tightened his fingers around her hand and leaned closer. He had no idea what she would remember or how she would feel. Hell, he had no idea of her medical state at all.

He *did* know that he would be there for her. Support her through whatever she was feeling, physically, mentally, and emotionally.

Maya's eyes fluttered open. They immediately went wide, riddled with anxiety. Her head pivoted to face him. The moment their gazes clashed, some of the anxiety was replaced with relief.

"Bodie..."

He breathed his first deep breath in twelve hours. Her gentle voice was everything. "Hi there, sweetheart." With his free hand,

Bodie moved stray hairs from her face, grazing the softness of her skin with his finger. "You have no idea how glad I am to see those beautiful eyes."

From the moment she'd gone missing, he'd been so damn worried. It had been an agony more intense than any he'd ever felt. And seeing that syringe in her chest…His world had stopped.

A small frown married her brows. Then her hand flew to her chest. "The needle—"

The door to their room opened, causing Maya to go silent. Wyatt and Oliver stepped inside. Neither looked like they were about to drop some bad news on them. Hopefully, that meant they'd found some *good* news.

"Hey there, darlin'. How you feeling?" Oliver asked in a gentle tone.

The edges of her lips lifted slightly, like she was trying to smile but couldn't quite get there yet. "Not too bad, I think. I mean, I feel some odd aches and pains from what happened in the woods," Bodie's jaw tightened at the reminder, "but recently, I've been waking up with a tight chest and some shortness of breath. I don't feel any of that right now."

Neither Oliver nor Wyatt seemed surprised by Maya's words. In fact, they actually had smiles on their faces. Like they knew something Maya and Bodie didn't.

"Did you find out about Maya's condition?" he asked, even though his gut already told him they had.

"Yes." Wyatt's brows creased as he scratched his head. "That drug Sinclair gave you clotted the hole in your heart."

Air whooshed out of Bodie's chest. That was exactly what he wanted to hear. What he'd been *praying* to hear. The relief was almost overwhelming.

"The scans barely show where the hole was, actually," Wyatt continued.

He heard Maya's quick intake of breath. "How is that possible?"

Oliver chuckled. "That's funny. It's exactly what the doctors are asking out there. The shock on their faces actually made me laugh. Not often you see a bunch of smart people looking confused."

Bodie was shocked too, and he didn't even work in the medical profession. Everything he'd read said that if the hole was too big to close on its own, surgery was the only option.

"The drug he pushed into your heart formed a gel-like structure and found the hole. Then it turned solid." Wyatt looked as stunned as Bodie felt. "Everyone's both shocked and impressed. But I shouldn't be too surprised. If Project Arma can turn men like us into whatever the hell we are, clotting a hole in the heart isn't a stretch."

Oliver's smile widened. "They're saying that this could be a major medical breakthrough. Could help a lot of people."

It was about time something good came from Arma.

Bodie lifted Maya's hand and pressed a kiss to her skin. "Thank god for that."

"I don't know what to say," Maya said softly. "I wasn't expecting to survive."

The muscles in Bodie's body tightened. She had expected to die. The knowledge was like a physical blow.

Oliver shoved his hands in his pockets. "Well, we're done delivering the good news. We'll wait in the hall."

"Quinn's just grabbing coffees from the cafeteria. She should be back in a couple of minutes." Wyatt shook his head. "Usually, I tease her about her coffee obsession, but she's been up all night, so I'll let this one slide."

Maya chuckled. It was music to Bodie's ears.

Oliver and Wyatt stepped out of the room. When it was just the two of them again, Maya's expression sobered. "What happened to Sinclair and the doctor?"

"They're both dead."

Maya closed her eyes and sighed. There was so much relief in that sound. "It's over."

It wasn't over. Not yet. Sinclair was but one piece of the Project Arma puzzle. But at least they'd eliminated another chunk of Hylar's team. They'd weakened him even further. And they would continue to weaken him until the man had nothing. Then they would destroy him.

MAYA STEPPED into Inwood Bar and immediately wanted to cry. The place looked nothing like it had a week ago. The explosion had turned the middle half of the bar into ash and blown out the wall between the bar area and the kitchen. A significant amount of roof and flooring was black.

Bodie's arm tightened around her waist, and he pressed a kiss to her temple.

"This is our fault," Maya whispered.

"No." Bodie shook his head. "This is not your fault or mine. This is a hundred percent Sinclair's."

Maybe. But Maya was the one who'd decided to come here. Now, because of Trish's kindness in employing Maya, the woman's bar was destroyed.

Footsteps sounded from the hall before Trish stepped into view. When her eyes landed on them, Maya half expected to see anger. Maybe even disappointment.

She saw neither of those things.

The older woman sighed before crossing the room and pulling Maya into her arms. It took a moment for Maya to snap out of her shock and hug the woman back.

"I am so darn happy that you're okay, girl." Trish pulled away but held on to Maya's arms. "You scared the crap out of me, missy. When the firefighters finally got everything under control and you and Bodie were missing, I just about lost my mind."

Maya's brows creased together. "Weren't you worried about your bar—"

Trish scoffed. "The bar is a physical structure. It and everything in it can be replaced. That's what insurance is for. You can't be replaced."

Maya's chest heated at her kind words.

Trish studied her face. "How are you?"

"I'm okay." Better than okay, actually. She had a fully intact heart now. A heart that was also full of love, thanks to the wonderful man beside her.

"Good. I can't believe that no-good ex of yours threatened Tina with deportation if she didn't blow up the bar. That's a whole new level of psychopath."

Maya gave a tight nod.

Trish had been told part truth and part lie. Tina *had* been threatened with deportation for her and her mother if she didn't set off the bomb in the bar. But of course, the threat had come from Sinclair, not an ex.

They still didn't know the exact details of how it all happened so quickly. Barely any time had passed between them handing in their resignation, Tina being hired, and that fateful explosion. The only thing they could assume was that Sinclair must have been watching. Watching the bar and everyone who came and went. Being in the CIA, he also had connections. People who could do background checks and find information to be used against a person.

Truth be told, Maya felt sorry for Tina. She'd become unfairly entangled in this mess. To protect herself and her mother, she'd been forced to do something terrible, and was now paying the price.

At the sound of the door opening, Maya turned her head to see Roe entering. He joined them, studying Maya with an intensity she hadn't quite seen on his face before. "You okay?"

She nodded. "I'm okay."

Roe looked at Bodie. She saw him nod from her peripheral vision.

Roe nodded back. "Good. They catch the asshole?"

"Yes," Bodie answered before Maya could.

He was silent for a moment before nodding once again. Then he turned to Trish. "My usual, please."

Maya had to laugh. "There's only half a bar left and you're still coming in?"

The man didn't so much as pause as he took a seat. "Yep. There's still Trish and there's still beer."

Maya understood. This was the guy's second home. Truth be told, this place had become a bit of a home to Maya, too. She was going to miss it. Not the bar, but the people.

Maya and Bodie stuck around for another couple of minutes, chatting. Shayna popped in during that time and also said a goodbye. The goodbyes were hard. So much harder than she'd expected.

Her heart was full though. The people she'd met in the last few months had all helped to heal her.

When they stepped out, Bodie took Maya's hand as they headed to the car. "How far is Marble Falls again?" she asked.

"Far enough that a plane is needed. Not so far that we can't come back and visit."

That didn't sound so bad. "Often?"

Maya wanted to make visiting these people—this town—a regular occurrence. With Bodie by her side, of course.

Bodie released her hand and wrapped his arm around her waist. "Once we've caught Hylar, we can visit as often as you like."

God, she loved him. "I'm going to miss them." After being alone for so long, finally having people around who cared about her was a new and wonderful feeling. But she knew they couldn't stay. Bodie needed to be in Marble Falls. He'd become the single-most important person in her life, so she chose him. Just like she'd always choose him.

"I know. I'm sorry we have to leave. I'm excited for you to meet the rest of my team though. I know I've said this before, but everyone's going to love you."

She was a bit nervous, especially about meeting the men. They were so important to Bodie that she wanted to make a good impression.

Quinn, Oliver, and Wyatt were all amazing. If the rest of the team was anything like them, she didn't think she had anything to worry about.

They stopped at the car, but when Maya reached for the handle, Bodie put pressure on her hips to turn her around. "I don't know if I've told you this, but you're amazing. The way you took on Sinclair. Ran and fought for your life…"

She leaned into him. Absorbing his warmth and strength. "Thank you. But I think you're the amazing one, Bodie. Thank you for coming for me."

"I'll always come for you."

Lowering his head, he touched his lips to hers. The loneliness that had become a constant companion in her life was no longer there. Bodie had replaced it with his love and his unwavering commitment.

CHAPTER 30

*O*liver threw his head back and laughed at Kye's retelling of the previous night. A real belly laugh, which had his problems momentarily disappearing.

God, it was good to be home. They'd only arrived back in Marble Falls a few days ago. The impromptu team catchup was exactly what he needed.

Or, more accurately, the family catchup.

These were the moments he lived for. Moments when he was surrounded by his closest friends, cold beer in hand and laugher floating around the room. They sat around on the mats in the training area of their business, Marble Protection. The sanctuary they'd built from the ground up. It made the night that much sweeter.

Maya was sitting between Quinn and Bodie. The smile on her face evidence of her happiness.

Oliver was glad. He had a soft spot for the woman. She had impressed the hell out of him with the way she'd fought off Sinclair and forced the guy to chase her through the woods. She was tough.

What was more, she made Bodie happy. *All* the women

around him made his brothers happy. Some might consider all the love and connection in the room a weakness. Hylar definitely did.

They didn't.

Oliver had seen firsthand the way love made a man strong rather than soft. It made him twice the protector.

Not that being single was a bad thing. Far from it. Oliver anticipated he would be single for a long time. Who knew, he might even be single forever. And he didn't feel one bit of unease about it.

Before Bodie had met Maya, he'd been wanting to find love. Openly talking about it with his brothers. Oliver didn't feel that. Did he love women? Hell, yes, he did. That didn't mean he felt the need to commit to one for the rest of his life.

Bodie stood, beer in hand, and made his way across the room, taking a seat beside Oliver. "Hey, brother, how you doing?"

"Good. Keystone was nice, but being home is...well, you know."

"I do." Bodie took a swig of his beer. "I don't think I've said thank you yet."

Oliver frowned. "Why would you need to thank me?"

"For traveling to Keystone and having my back. Having Maya's back."

Oliver was shaking his head before his friend had finished speaking. "You don't need to thank me. You know that. We're all in this together."

Not just because they were basically brothers, but also because they were stronger as a unit. Separately, they were weapons. Together they were an army. They would use that to their advantage against every enemy.

Bodie ran a hand through his hair. "Damn, I'm glad to have you guys."

Oliver clamped a hand on his shoulder. "You and me both."

His gaze shot across the room to Maya. "I'm happy for you that you found your woman."

Bodie immediately looked toward her. "It's strange. A couple months ago, when Wyatt said we needed someone to watch her, I knew it should be me. It sounds crazy. I had no idea who she was. It's almost like the universe knew she was mine before we'd even met."

That wasn't crazy. That was damn beautiful. The man deserved every minute of his happiness.

"You deserve it, brother. I hope all your days are this happy."

Some of the light dimmed from Bodie's eyes. "Me too."

Oliver knew what he was thinking about. Hylar. Carter. The danger that still existed in their world. The danger that stalked them.

"One day, we'll be safe." Oliver knew that with very real clarity.

"One day soon," Bodie whispered. His eyes didn't leave Maya. "You thought any more about that woman?"

A smile tugged at Oliver's lips. "Her name was Tori. And not really. I'm a lone wolf, remember?"

"You don't have to be."

Oliver took a sip of his beer. "I love you, buddy, but you and I are very different people when it comes to this stuff."

Bodie's lips pulled into a smile, almost like he knew a secret that Oliver didn't. "Maybe. Or maybe you're just not there yet."

Ah, hell. If he was going to listen to his loved-up friends for the rest of the night, he was going to need another beer…or ten.

Oliver lifted his almost empty bottle. "I'm going to get another."

He pushed to his feet.

It wasn't like Tori hadn't been in his thoughts. Hell, who could forget those sky-blue eyes and that cute-as-heck laugh? But he'd been telling Bodie the truth. He wasn't looking for love. His mind was on Hylar and danger and the damn project.

Oliver had just grabbed a bottle from the fridge behind the front counter when his gaze snagged on something through the glass front door. Or more accurately, *someone*. Standing across the street.

Ordinarily, that wouldn't be noteworthy. But considering it was both pitch-black out there and raining? Yeah, he noticed. Then a frown pulled at his brows and he took a small step toward the door...

Tori?

Placing the beer on the counter, Oliver was halfway to the exit when Kye stepped in front of him.

"Ax! Where the hell are you going? Was my reenactment of last Saturday night so bad you have to leave?"

"Just getting some fresh air." Oliver started to step around Kye, distracted, but his friend gripped his arm. All signs of joking faded as Kye took a step closer.

"Hey, you okay?"

He was fine. Just a bit concerned about the woman standing outside, getting drenched. He didn't have time to explain to his friend.

"I'm great. Just need a break from all the love in the room."

That was something Kye would be able to understand.

His friend's lips stretched. "I know that feeling. Want company?"

"Nah, I'm okay. I won't be long."

He actually had no idea how long he'd be. Finding out why she was standing in the dark, in the rain, was at the top of his priority list. Getting her dry and warm was also up there.

"Gotcha." Kye headed back to the group.

Oliver pushed outside, stepping onto the sidewalk. The rain hit him as he searched the street.

Empty.

What the hell? Had he imagined her being out there?

He scrubbed a hand over his face. God, he needed to get a

grip. He'd hardly slept since getting back from Keystone. He'd hardly slept *in* Keystone. His mind was consumed with everything the team needed to accomplish. And now he was hallucinating women.

Christ, he was losing it.

Oliver shot one more glance in both directions before heading back inside.

Tonight, he needed to sleep for a solid eight hours. Then maybe he could search for Hylar with a little more focus, instead of wasting time standing in the rain, searching for a woman he'd spent a single night with.

Order Oliver today!

ALSO BY NYSSA KATHRYN

PROJECT ARMA SERIES

(Series Ongoing)

Uncovering Project Arma

Luca

Eden

Asher

Mason

Wyatt

Bodie

Oliver

Kye

JOIN my newsletter at www.nyssakathryn.com and be the first to find
out about sales and new releases!

ABOUT THE AUTHOR

Nyssa Kathryn is a romantic suspense author. She lives in South Australia with her daughter and hubby and takes every chance she can to be plotting and writing. Always an avid reader of romance novels, she considers alpha males and happily-ever-afters to be her jam.

Don't forget to follow Nyssa and never miss another release.

Facebook | Instagram | Amazon | Goodreads

DEC   2022

CPSIA information can be obtained
at www.ICGtesting.com
Printed in the USA
BVHW082254130222
628954BV00002B/188

9 780648 946250